"Whit, you didn't come here for the girls."

He stopped stoking the fire and looked at her. "What do you mean?"

"You came for me."

She went to him. His expression questioned what she was doing, but she couldn't answer. She didn't know what she was doing. For sure, she wasn't seducing him; her ex-fiancé had erased any aggressive sexual ideas from her head. But Whit...

She'd seen how he looked at her. Knew he'd been celibate since his wife's death. Knew his girls dominated his time.

But when she put her arms around his neck, a groan escaped him, more primal than a wolf's cry.

Just like that she knew what Whit wanted for Christmas. And she was the only one who could give it to him.

THE BONUS MUM

BY
JENNIFER GREENE

First published in Great Britain 2013
by Mills & Boon, an imprint of Harlequin (UK) Limited,
Eton House, 18-24 Paradise Road, Richmond, Surrey TW9 1SR

© Alison Hart 2013

ISBN: 978 0 263 90146 7
ebook ISBN: 978 1 472 00534 2

23-0913

Harlequin (UK) policy is to use papers that are natural, renewable and recyclable products and made from wood grown in sustainable forests. The logging and manufacturing processes conform to the legal environmental regulations of the country of origin.

Printed and bound in Spain
by Blackprint CPI, Barcelona

Jennifer Greene lives near Lake Michigan with her husband and an assorted menagerie of pets. Michigan State University has honored her as an outstanding woman graduate for her work with women on campus. Jennifer has written more than seventy love stories, for which she has won numerous awards, including four RITA® Awards from the Romance Writers of America and their Hall of Fame and Lifetime Achievement Awards.

You're welcome to contact Jennifer through her website at www.jennifergreene.com.

To the real "Lilly,"
who is likely to get a zillion more dedications
from me. You're the light of our lives, sweetheart!

Chapter One

When the oven bell dinged, Rosemary sprinted for the kitchen faster than the sound of a fire alarm. She'd added a ton of amenities to the old MacKinnon lodge in the past six months, but a new stove never made the budget. The temperature gauge in the oven could be downright cantankerous.

This time, thankfully, the old monster behaved. She grabbed a hot pad and pulled out a tray of cream puffs, all swelled up, their surface a golden-brown. Perfect.

While the puffs cooled, she headed outside to cart in an armload of peachwood. Outside, a blustery wind bit her face with needles, but considering it was December 19, Rosemary figured she was lucky. There could be snow or a serious ice storm on top of Whisper Mountain by now. A little wind was nothing.

Back inside, she knelt in front of the massive fieldstone fireplace. The grate already had a huge bed of snapping, orange coals, just needed a stir and a poke and fresh logs. Moments later, she had a sassy crackle of fire back, warming the whole living room.

She stood up and stretched, dusting her hands. The MacKinnons had spent a lot of Christmases here when she was a kid. She couldn't remember the last holiday when the place hadn't been a complete wreck. By now, there should be a giant Christmas tree in the corner, already dropping needles. Dusty Santas and holiday tchotchkes should be cluttering every surface. Instead, there was no tree, no winking lights, no tinsel or glitter, no wrapping paper and crushed bows anywhere in sight. The place was fabulously tidy and clean.

Truth to tell…she hated it. She had no problem working alone, being alone. But darn it, at this time of year she loved the chaos, the clutter, the razzle-dazzle, the messes, the feasts and for darned sure, the time with her family.

This year she just couldn't do it. So…she'd decided to ignore the holiday altogether. She'd work, and when she got sick of work, she planned a heap of silly distractions.

Like wasting time on *Judge Judy* and old sappy movies.

Like having cream puffs for dinner—with vanilla bean ice cream and hot, dark chocolate sauce. And cherries.

She foraged for a big spoon, and had just pulled the steaming-cold container of ice cream from the freezer when the front door suddenly blasted open. She went to the kitchen doorway, figuring she must not have adequately latched the front door—but that wasn't the issue at all. Over the wheeze and whistle of wind came the unmistakable sound of screams and cries. Human screams and cries. Girls. Children. Dozens of children, judging from the volume of cries.

She dropped the spoon, dropped the ice cream, peeled out of the kitchen.

There were children. Not a herd of them, just two girls, red-faced and shaking and crying.

They spotted her, and as if identifying a woman was all it took to let go, thundered toward her in a nonstop sputter of tears and words.

"You have to help us! There's a bear chasing us! A huge *grizzly* bear! He wants to kill us!"

"He's right *out* there. We ran and ran. I ran so hard my side hurt and I still kept going—"

"We didn't know where we were going. Anywhere. We just had to keep running because it kept coming after us!"

"It's still out there! It could still get us!"

"You think it could break windows? It was huge! I thought we were going to die!"

"And what if there's more than one? What if that bear was *married* and there's a wife, too, and he has baby bears only they're all big like that—?"

Rosemary raised her hands, and finally managed to squeeze in a few words. "Hold it. You're both safe. No bear is getting in here. Let's get your coats off, sit down by the fire. I want to hear the whole story, everything you want to say, but let's calm it down a few octaves, okay?"

They'd closed the front door—slammed it, actually, and she bolted it. The front closet had a shotgun, locked on the top shelf. The girls' jaws dropped when they saw it.

"Are you going to kill the bear?"

"Afraid I'm not much on killing anything. But I'm going to shoot a couple blasts in the air. There's a good chance he'll scare off."

"Oh. Can we watch?"

"You can watch from the window. I'm guessing neither one of you are in a hurry to go back outside this minute, right?"

"Oh. Right."

She looked outside, both north and east windows, before opening the door. If a bear had been close—seriously close—she would have smelled it. Nothing smelled quite like a wild bear. She didn't want to steal the girls' thunder by telling them grizzlies didn't live anywhere near Whisper Mountain, South Carolina. Besides, black bears definitely did. They usually snoozed through the cold months, but never went into total hibernation. She stepped outside, clicked off the safety, and aimed a shot at the sky. Then a second one.

She was only gone for a minute—max—but when she stepped back in and relocked the door, the girls were sitting on the old leather couch, staring at her openmouthed.

"Something tells me you girls weren't raised in the country," she said wryly.

That started them talking again. They came from Charleston. Their dad had taken them out of school a little early and rented this place on the mountain. They were doing the whole holiday here. It was because their mom had died about a year ago. Just before Christmas. She'd been Christmas shopping with them. A big truck hit her. Their mom died and both girls ended up in the hospital. They'd missed a heap of school, and Pepper had two casts, and Lilly really wrecked her left foot and had some scars, but not so much now. Anyway, their dad thought it'd be hard to have Christmas at home this year, because it was like an anniversary from when their mom died, so they were here. Having fun mostly. Until the bear.

Rosemary took in this information between handing out drinks and waiting through bathroom breaks.

At some point, one of them wandered toward the kitchen, and that started them on a different track. One picked up the dropped ice cream container, the other honed straight for the cream puffs. They immediately confessed that they'd never had a cream puff and didn't think they could live another minute before trying one. They were desperately hungry. It was from all that running away from the vicious, angry bear.

One of them abruptly realized that they should have phoned their dad right off—and promptly took out a cell. The line was busy, but that wasn't a problem, because their dad never talked on the phone long, and rather than leave him a message that they'd been in terrible danger because of the bear, they figured they'd just call him in another couple minutes.

Rosemary's ears were ringing by then...but she'd more or less sorted them out. They were twins. Eleven. Lilly and Pepper. They were both blonde, both coltish and lanky. They both had straight, fine hair, shoulder length, but one had a red streak and the other had a green one. They had purple jackets that matched, skinny jeans, blue eyes…but not identical blue eyes. Lilly's were uniquely blue, with a dark ring around the light blue iris—the effect was mesmerizing and striking. Pepper had a tendency to scrunch up her nose and prance around, restless, curious, irrepressible.

They were both cute.

They were both going to be breathtaking.

Rosemary figured once they left, she was going to need a long nap. After they'd finished talking, they started on her with questions. How come she lived here? She *really* studied orchids? What was a university grant? So was she wearing a Duke sweatshirt because that's where she got the grant? She *really* had her own gun? Oh, my God, was that a dark room, and could she develop pictures by herself? Could they see? Was she married? Well, if she wasn't married, what was she doing for Christmas?

"Wait a minute. You can't spend Christmas alone," Lilly said firmly.

Right about then Rosemary suggested they call their father again.

Pepper grabbed the cell phone from Lilly—they only had one cell phone between them, which apparently caused arguments several times a day. This time their dad promptly answered, and Pepper went on a long rendition of the walk, the bear, the bear chase, the house, Rosemary, the cream puffs.

"Can you come and get us, Dad? We really got lost when we started running. And now it's already dark, even though it's so early…. I told you, we're at Rosemary's. Oh. Well, no, I…" Pepper lifted the phone and arched her brows to Rosemary. "Could you tell my dad where we are?"

Rosemary was almost laughing as she pressed the cell to her ear. Pepper had a ditsy side, for sure. She'd sounded as if she assumed her dad had some magical ability to automatically know where she was.

"Hi— I'm Rosemary MacKinnon," she said immediately.

"And I'm Whit Cochran."

She took a quick breath. He just had one of those unique guy voices, a clear tenor, that put a shiver in her pulse. It didn't matter if he was ugly as sin or plain as a sloth—she had no way to know, and didn't care. It was just that his voice made her think of sex and danger. Preferably together.

"Just tell me quick," he started with. "Are the girls hurt in any way? And are they okay now?"

"They're fine—except for conning me out of ice cream probably before they've had dinner."

"There really was a bear?"

"I didn't see it myself, but black bears regularly wander around here. Normally they don't bother humans, but they'll venture close when they're scrounging for food. At this time of year, it's pretty rare to come across one."

"I like your voice, Rosemary MacKinnon."

The comment was so unexpected, she got an inexcusable warm fuzzy feeling in her tummy…but obviously, she'd relieved his mind about his girls and he was just getting his breath back, not thinking clearly. "I'm guessing you'd like my address," she said quickly.

"Yes, of course."

"You're not far. There aren't that many places near the top of Whisper Mountain. I'm on the east side, and most of the land up here is MacKinnon property. I'd guess you're either in the Landers place or the Stewarts...they often rent out at Christmas. The Stewarts' place is brick, double kitchen, double deck—"

"That's the one."

"So. If you're driving a car, you're going to have to go down the mountain road—there's only one, as you probably know. Where it ends in a Y shape, turn left. Give or take a half mile, you'll see a wood sign for MacKinnons—that'll lead to the house here. Take you ten, fifteen minutes. On the other hand, if you have some way to go cross-country—"

"A Gator."

"Okay, so it's your choice...with the Gator, you go up that same mountain road...you'll run into a gravel road, turn right, then zip along that way until you run into a battered old MacKinnon sign, turn in."

"So the girls really weren't far."

"I don't know...they could have circled and back-tracked a zillion times if they were trying to outrun a bear. Speaking of which...until you get here, I'll be talking bear defense with your girls."

"Maybe you'd better have that talk with me, too."

She laughed, so did he...but when she clicked off the phone, she found both girls sitting side by side on the leather couch, staring at her.

"Your dad'll be here in two shakes." When they kept up with the stare, she cocked her head. "What?"

"You laughed. And we thought we heard Dad laughing."

Rosemary didn't understand. "He did laugh. But not because he thought your bear was funny. He had to hear that you two were safe. So he was relieved, and naturally he got in a happier mood."

Lilly said, "Our dad hasn't done a whole lot of laughing since Mom died."

She didn't know what to say. The girls had already spilled a lot of information about their personal circumstances that was none of her business. She didn't want to pry—but actually, she was relieved to understand their circumstances. She could have said something painful or insensitive accidentally, if she'd never known the girls had lost their mom, and that they were trying to have a different kind of Christmas to keep the grieving memories at bay.

"Hey. Should we call you Mrs. MacKinnon? Or Miss MacKinnon? Or Rosemary? Or what?" Lilly was clearly the one who wanted to know the rules.

"You can call me Rosemary. And I'm a Miss, not a Mrs."

"How come?" That was definitely Pepper. No boundaries on Pepper's tongue.

"Because I was happy being single."

"Oh. Okay. Can we look around, while we're waiting for my dad? It's about the most beautiful house I can remember."

"Yes, you can look around…except in the first room down that hall. For a long time it was a utility room, but I turned it into a dark room to develop photographs. When that door's closed, you'll see a red light next to the knob, and that means you shouldn't open the door."

"You really develop pictures? Yourself? Right here?"

It had been a while since she'd "awestruck" any-one…much less had anyone treat her like a goddess. Her family—at least her parents—rarely had a pleasant word to say to her. Since June, whenever they called, it was invariably to make sure she knew her Terrible Mistake hadn't been forgotten, and probably never would be. Her two brothers would have defended her against the world—and always had—but even they skirted around the question of why she'd done such a "damn fool thing."

The girls talked her ears off—and asked more questions than a teacher on a test. But after being raised with two brothers—and working alone all these months since June—Rosemary didn't mind. She inhaled all the girl talk.

She never heard a knock on the door, never heard anything until the girls both squealed, *"Dad!"*

They'd ended up in the kitchen—both girls had chosen to ignore the table, and instead sat on the counter with their legs swinging—some body part *always* seemed to be in motion with them. They'd somehow conned her into wrapping up three more cream puffs to take home with them. Possibly she'd been easily conned. Besides, she'd made the full recipe, and even sugar-greedy as she was, couldn't possibly eat a dozen.

"Dad! We're having so much *fun!* Can we stay a little longer?"

And then, "Dad, this is Rosemary. Rosemary, this is Dad—"

"He's not Dad when you're introducing him, dummy.

He's Whit. Dad, this is Rosemary. Rosemary, this is Whit. *Wait* until you taste these cream puffs! Rosemary's giving us some to take home."

"She has a darkroom, Dad. And she has a *gun*. A big *rifle*. That she *owns*. It's all hers. Everything!"

Over the bouncingly exuberant girls, their eyes met. She was both laughing and rolling her eyes—there was no shutting the girls up, no chance to temper their exuberance. And his eyes were filled with humor, too....

But somehow she'd expected the girls' father to be... well, fatherly looking. A lot older than her twenty-seven. Sure, she'd expected him to be reasonably good-looking, because the girls were adorable, but he'd been married awhile. He should have looked more staid, the way settled down guys tended to get, more safe, less... how would a woman say it?...less hungry.

Whit radiated all the safety of a cougar just freed from a cage. He was tall, rangy and sleek. He had the shoulder and arm muscles of a guy who was physical and exceptionally strong. He wore an old canvas jacket, jeans and country boots.

His hair was sort of a dusty blond shade, rumpled from the wind, a frame for the rugged bones in his face. The haircut was the choice for a guy who didn't waste time on grooming. Straight eyebrows set off his eagle-shrewd eyes—shrewd, except when he looked at his daughters.

Then his gaze turned into a helpless puppy's.

"Did they drive you crazy?" He said it under the relentless stream of eleven-year-old chatter.

Oh, right. Like she'd kick a puppy in the teeth. The

girls were obviously the sun and the moon to him. Besides, even if they had driven her a little crazy, they'd been fun. "They're wonderful," she said.

"Yeah. I think so. But…"

"I never had a chance to give them the 'bear' talk. They should know…you don't run from a bear. You don't leave food in the wild, ever, and if you make loud noises, he'll likely turn tail and take off. A bear doesn't want to hurt a human—unless it's spring and it's a female with cubs. Or it's fall, and he's filling up on every berry he can find. So if they spot one from a distance, just move away. Make noise. Trust me, he doesn't want to eat you. He just wants you out of his space."

Pepper had been listening, but she wasn't buying this advice wholesale. "But what if he's crazy? You know. What if it's a people-hater bear. Like the bear in that movie, where the model's in Alaska—"

"If he's crazy, you're up a creek. But the population of black bears around here doesn't have a bad reputation. If a crazy one showed on the radar, DNR and rangers would be all over it. So if you just use common sense and do the regular safe things, you should be fine."

"Dad, do you see how much she knows? Even about things like bears? And she's a girl."

"I noticed that."

Her head whipped toward him again. There was nothing suggestive in his tone. Just in his eyes. There was just something there that sparked a sizzle in her pulse…and Rosemary was too darned practical to feel sizzles—in her pulse or anywhere else.

"I think it's time we got out of this nice lady's hair."

"But she likes us, Dad. She said so."

"Of course she likes you. You're the angels of the universe. But we're still giving Rosemary her life back and going home. It's already dark."

"You sure didn't call us angels when we put the red and green in our hair. Even though we told you and told you and told you it'd wash out. And everybody does it."

The adults barely exchanged another word—they had no chance. Rosemary was amused—and surprised—by the violent silence when she closed the door after them. She was used to silence. Or she should be. She was happy living alone.

Or that's what she'd been telling herself for six months now.

Maybe she'd been telling herself that her whole life. If you're waiting for someone else to make you happy, you're waiting for a spit in the wind. It has to start on the inside. Being content with who you are.

Rosemary always thought she was. Content within herself. Until last June, and since then she couldn't seem to fit in her own skin.

She turned away from the window, fed the fire and turned her attention back to things that mattered. Another cream puff, for starters.

And what a hunk of a man that Whit was. Maybe she could have a hot, steamy dream about him tonight. He was the kind of guy that looked all sexy and dangerous when he was sweaty.

Not that Rosemary was attracted to sweat and oiled shoulders and bad boys.

But losing a wife and raising two young girls alone—

that was a tough road. Tougher than her own problems, by far.

Which was probably why she couldn't get him off her mind.

Chapter Two

Whit opened the refrigerator and stared at it blankly. He'd bought a truckful of groceries. The fridge was full. He just couldn't seem to find anything to eat.

At least anything that didn't involve cooking and dishes and cleaning up.

"What are you hungry for, you two?" He called out to the living room, and then wondered why he'd asked.

The answer came in joyous unison. "Mac and cheese. From the box."

Followed by, "And don't burn it this time, Dad."

He still had two boxes, thank God. All the green stuff he'd bought was going to waste. But the sugary cereals, the mac and cheese and the ice cream—after two days, he was nearly out of those. He could probably feed the kids on five bucks a day—if they had their way. Instead he'd spent better than $500 on stuff that was good for them.

Why wasn't that in the parenting rule book, huh? That short of putting an eleven-year-old in a coma, there was no way to get anything fresh and green down them without a war that involved pouting, door slamming, dramatic tragic looks, claims of being misunderstood, claims of being adopted, claims of child abuse…and… that torture could go on for hours. Sometimes days.

He scrounged for a pan, and filled it with water. Read the directions on the mac and cheese box for the millionth time. When he turned around, Lilly was leaning on the blue-and-white tile counter.

It was a trick, since he knew she hadn't come in to help. He was in trouble. He just didn't know over what. And the truth—which Lilly possibly knew—was that he'd do anything she asked. Anything.

He was terrified of both daughters, but Lilly more than Pepper. Lilly had stopped talking after her mom died. She'd just lain there, in that hospital bed next to her sister, but where Pepper would cry and shriek, Lilly just carried that silent look in her eyes. Grief too deep to understand, grief that made her go still, as if in any motion, no matter how tiny, could tip her over the edge. She couldn't take more.

Eventually Lilly started talking again, but it went on and on, that grief of hers. She answered questions, and talked about things like school and dinner, but it was months before she volunteered anything. Months before that unbearably sharp grief started to fade. Months before he won a real smile—and he'd done everything but stand on his head and grovel, to bring her beautiful smile back.

"What?" he said, when she kept leaning there, looking at him, kind of rolling her shoulders.

"Nothing. I was just thinking...."

That was the other problem with Lilly. Pepper, thankfully, said anything that was on her mind. It came out like froth; he never had to work to figure out where her head was. But Lilly was the thinker, the one who stored hurts on the inside, the one who never said anything he could anticipate. Nothing in the universe could make him feel as helpless as Lilly.

And he'd have to kill anyone who dared cause her any grief again.

"Didn't you think she was pretty?" She asked him as if his answer was of no consequence, while idly scratching the back of one knee with a slipper.

"The lady?"

"Rosemary, Dad. You heard her name. And yeah. Didn't you think she was pretty?"

"Sure."

Lilly rolled her eyes. It was a default response when Whit did something inadequate on an eleven-year-old's terms. "Something's wrong with her."

"Like what?"

"I don't know. But she's pretty. And she's spending Christmas all by herself. And she's working, she showed us some stuff on orchids. But you'd think it was July or June or something. There's no tree or presents. No stuff. No lights."

"Maybe she's of some other religion."

"You mean like Buddhist or Muslim or something? No. It's not that."

"How do you know?"

"Because I know." Another default answer, usually accompanied by, "I'm a girl and I know. You wouldn't understand."

"Maybe she's Jewish?"

"Dad. We know five Jewish people. And they do Christmas with presents and trees just like we do. Except that they get to do their Hanukkah holiday, too, so they get even *more* presents. In fact, I was thinking about turning Jewish."

"Were you?"

"Hey, people fight wars all the time over religion. I think they should stop fighting wars and concentrate more on giving presents. Especially presents for their kids." Possibly out of boredom, she plucked a raw carrot from the glass of carrots and celery on the counter. It was the first time he'd seen her eat anything nutritious since they'd come up here. "But back to Rosemary. The thing is…she's our neighbor. In fact, as far as I can tell, she's our only neighbor up here. At least the only one we know about. So maybe we should do some Christmas stuff with her, so she's not alone."

"Honey, she may be alone by choice. She may not want company or neighbors around."

"Well, then, why were her eyes sad?"

The water started to swirl and bubble. He dumped in the dry pasta, asked Lilly to get some milk and butter from the fridge and called Pepper to set the table. Then he did what he always did when he needed a diversion. He called dibs on the TV as of eight o'clock.

That immediately raised the decibel level in the great room to rock concert levels…and for sure, diverted Lilly.

But Rosemary's face flashed back in his mind. She *did* have sad eyes. At first…well, at very first, he'd only seen his girls, because he'd nearly had a heart attack about their bear encounter. No matter what they'd claimed on the phone, he had to see them both in flesh and blood to breathe again.

Still, the minute he realized the kids were both fine, he swiftly turned on Rosemary. First, he noticed her vibrancy. With three females in the same room, naturally all three of them were talking at once, with volume, and were all in constant motion besides. But over and above his twins' chatter, he caught…the energy of her. The life-lover zest.

Her build was lithe and lean, a woman comfortable with her body, used to doing physical things and spending time outdoors. Even in December her nose had a hint of sunburn, with a thin spray of freckles.

Her eyes were faded blue, the color of a hot sky in summer. She wore her hair grass-short and styled wash-and-wear, not all that much different than his, but no one would ever mistake her for a guy. Everything about her was soft and female. The long sleeved T-shirt in navy blue, the battered-soft jeans, the sculpted fine bones in her face. None of her clothes were fancy but distinctly feel-good styles, easy to move in, easy to live in. She wore no makeup—of course, since she lived alone, why would she paint her face? But it was more than that. Her skin had that wind-fresh, sun-friendly wholesome look. Her breasts were small and pert; her hips barely held up her jeans. There was no vanity in her. No embellishments. Just…beauty.

The real kind of beauty.

The kind that rang his chimes. Only no one—real or not—had rung his chimes since Zoe died.

Sooner or later, he figured he'd get his libido back. He'd always been overcharged, not under, but Zoe's death seemed to kill something off in him.

He'd never identified it that way. Never thought of it at all.

Yet one look at Rosemary, and his libido showed up and started singing bass. With drums.

And yeah, the sadness in her eyes touched him—maybe should have warned him. But that sadness wasn't *her.* It was about something that had happened to her. And...

"*Dad!* You're burning the mac and cheese again!"

He glanced down at the pot. How had that happened again?

By the time they sat down at the table, Whit realized that something was up. A father of twins learned some things the hard way. Two children were just two children—but twins were a pack. Like wolves. Or badgers.

Especially like badgers.

"Listen, Dad." Pepper shoveled in the mac and cheese, but took time to offer him a beguiling smile. She was always the troublemaker.

"I'm listening."

"We're really happy up here. It's awesome and all. And we know you want us to forget Mom this Christmas."

He frowned. "No. No, you two, not at all. I just thought this Christmas would be extra hard without your mom. By next year, we could do the holiday completely differently. Make a point of remembering your mom, in fact—like making some of her favorite holiday dishes. Remember her strawberry pie? Or putting the tree in the corner where she thought it looked best. I don't ever want you to forget your mom, I just—"

"Dad, wind it up." Pepper again, using her impatient tone. "We're okay with all that. You don't have to go on and on."

"But here's the thing." Lilly, always the pacifier, jumped in when she thought her sis was being abrasive. "We don't know Rosemary very well. But she's alone. And we're alone this Christmas, too. Like you said before, maybe we'd be an intrusion. But maybe not. I mean, what if we just—like when we're cutting down our own tree tomorrow—cut one down for her, too?"

Pepper started her fidgety thing, dropping a napkin, then her fork. "And then we could just bring her the tree—and see if we're in her way or if she really needs to work or something. Because maybe she really wants some company around. Especially us girl company. She *said* she loved girl talk."

"It's not just that," Lilly interrupted again. "You know when I was little—"

"As compared to your being an old lady now?"

"Quit it, Dad. We're having a talk. No joking."

"Okay, okay."

"When I was little, I remember the neighbor who came over for Christmas. Mom said she was alone because she lost her husband. So she asked her over for Christmas dinner. Mom said, and then you said, that Christmas isn't just about presents. It's about people being together. Sharing something good."

"Sometimes you two worry me. You have this tendency to use things I've said against me."

"Come on, Dad. We can take Rosemary a tree tomorrow, right?"

Whit couldn't imagine how they could just show up
at Rosemary's back door with a tree out of the complete blue. But at least temporarily, he couldn't figure
out a way to say no that would make sense to the girls.

Rosemary bent over the corkboard. Heaven knew
how she'd gotten hung up on the sex life of wild orchids
in South Carolina. The subject would undoubtedly bore
most people to tears. But when she needed her mind off
stress, she'd always been able to concentrate on work.

Her stomach growled. She ignored it. She was pretty
sure she'd ignored it a couple times before this.

It had taken quite a while to completely fill the corkboard on the coffee table. She'd pinned photos of local
orchids—and their names and location—until the entire
space was filled. Some of the names were so fun. Little
lady's Tresses. Small whorled pogonia. Yellow fringed
orchid. Crested coralroot. Downy rattlesnake plantain.

Absently, she picked up her coffee mug. It was cold,
and since it was also the last in the pot, it was thicker
than mud. She still swallowed a slug.

She'd never planned on turning into an egghead. It
was all sort of a mistake. When she'd cancelled the wedding, escaped from George (as she thought of it now) the
two-year grant from Duke had struck her as a godsend.
She could make a living—or enough of a living—and
seclude herself up here.

The goal hadn't been to get a Ph.D. She'd never

wanted a Ph.D. She just wanted to work so hard she could forget about everything else for a while. Until she put her head back together. Until she figured out what to do with her life. Until she could analyze exactly what had gone so bad, so wrong, with George.

Mostly she had to figure out how she could have been so stupid.

She leaned forward, studying the photo of the small whorled pogonia. A white lip hung above the five green leaves. The species was teensy. It was hard to find, hard to notice. And it was probably the rarest orchid near the eastern coastline—which made it one of her treasures.

That was the thing. It wasn't about academics. Or getting a Ph.D. It was about...survival. Why did some species fail and others thrive? How could a fragile, vulnerable orchid like this conceivably survive in such a hostile environment?

Not that she thought of herself as vulnerable. Or that she feared she couldn't survive the mess she was in.

It was just that everybody believed the old adage that only the strong survived. Because it always seemed to be true. Except with these fragile orchids.

There had to be a reason. A logical explanation. Something in delicate orchids that enabled them to survive, when far tougher species died out.

A sudden knock on the door almost made her jump sky-high. A spit of coffee landed on her sweatshirt; she set the mug down, went to the door.

The twins huddled together like bookends, a platter in their hands covered with tin foil. "Hi, Rosemary. We can't stay. We can't bother you."

"But we made some brownies to thank you for saving our lives yesterday."

Clearly their opening lines had been prepared.

"The brownies," Pepper added, "have some mints and some cherries on the inside. We didn't sample any of these, but we've made them this way before. Honest, they're really good. Although we usually put in marshmallows, only this time, we didn't have any marshmallows so we couldn't."

Lilly's turn. "We were trying to make it red and green on the inside. You know. Like to be Christmasy." She took a breath. "Dad said we absolutely can't bother you. So we're leaving right now, this very instant."

She noticed the golf cart behind them. Saw the hope on their faces, no matter what they said. "You can't even come in to sample a brownie? That's an awful lot for just me to eat by myself."

"I don't think we can. No matter how much we want to." Pepper let out a massive sigh.

"Hmm. What if I call your dad and asked him myself if you could stay awhile?"

"Oh." Both girls lit up like sparklers. "Yeah. If *you* call him, it'll be okay."

There ended her bubble of solitude. She called Whit first, so he knew the girls were safely with her, said they wanted to share a brownie with her, and she'd have the girls call when they were headed home. It wouldn't be long.

Just that short conversation invoked symptoms she'd suffered when she met him yesterday. It was as if she'd been exposed to a virus. She felt oddly achy and restless, hot—when there was no excuse in the universe to react like a dimwit toward a perfect stranger.

But the girls distracted her from thinking any more about their father. The first priority was testing the brownies—which were fabulous. Both girls could somehow eat and talk nonstop at the same time.

Pepper went first. "Our dad thought we couldn't handle Christmas at home. But we both know he's the one who can't. He hasn't been out one single time since mom died. You know what that means?"

Rosemary was afraid to answer. "How about if you tell me what you think it means."

"It means that he's trying to be there for us 24/7. Rosemary, he's driving us *nuts*. He wants us to *do* things together all the time."

"And that's bad?" She might not have a chance to think about Whit in connection with herself, but if the conversation was going to be all about him...well there's not much she can do about it. She reached for a second brownie, feeling self-righteous as the devil herself.

"It's not *bad*. Because we love him. But can you picture a pajama party with seven girls and my dad trying to fit in?"

"Um...no."

"Everybody in our class at school likes going to the movies. It's like a couple miles, though, so if the weather's good, we walk. Otherwise one of the moms drive. But Dad, when it was his turn, he wanted to go inside with us. He sat in the back. Like the kids wouldn't know he was there?"

"Um..." Rosemary eyed a third brownie.

"We know he's lonely. He really loved our mom.

He just can't seem to get over it. But it's been a *year*. I mean, we miss her, too."

Lilly said softly, "I think about her every day."

"I do, too!" Pepper said defensively.

"But really, we would have been fine just being home for Christmas. Then we could have had friends over. Or gone to their houses. See the Christmas movies and all that. So…" Lilly looked at her sister.

"So…" Pepper picked up the refrain.

"So…we were wondering if you would do some things with us. I don't mean every second, like when you have to work and stuff. But we're going to do a tree. And make some ornaments. Bake some cookies. It's stuff we're already *doing,* so we're not asking you to *work.* We'd just like you to be, well, another person."

"She *is* another person, stupid." Pepper, naturally.

"I *know* that, numbskull." Lilly turned to her again. "I meant, so Dad could see he didn't have to be hovering over us all the time. That it's okay. We're eleven. Practically adults. We don't need a parent in the same room with us every single minute."

"Besides, we want you there for ourselves. Because I'm sick of this hairstyle. And we've been arguing about how it'd look best. Lilly thinks we should both grow it way long. I think we should go short, and like, with spikes. You could help us with an opinion."

Lilly took her plate to the counter. "We wanted to bring you a tree. We're cutting down our tree tomorrow, so we told Dad, why don't we get one for Rosemary, too? But he said we had no way to know if you even wanted one. Don't you want a Christmas tree?"

Every direction she turned, she seemed to face the

gruesome problem of taking sides. And all their dad conversation was prickly—they kept relaying things that were private and none of her business. Even their enthusiasm at being around her was touchy—they were fun; she really wouldn't mind visits from them now and then. It wasn't as if she'd had a choice to spend the holiday alone. But Whit might not appreciate a stranger in the middle of their private holiday, no matter what the girls thought they wanted.

"Where did you get the golf cart?" she asked, hoping for a diversion.

"It was in the shed with the Gator. It came with the property. It'll go a few miles, like four or something, and then you just plug it back in. Dad won't let us drive the Gator, but he said we could use the cart to carry the brownies to your house and then come back."

"You weren't scared you'd run into your bear again?"

"A little. But we can go pretty fast in the cart. And we brought cookie sheets to make noise. We read a bunch about bears last night. Mostly it's like the stuff you told us. If a person doesn't do something that upsets him, the bear's really not interested in humans anyway." Pepper was about to jump up from the table, when her sister gave her a finger point. She rolled her eyes, but grabbed her dish and took it to the counter. "Anyhow, I know we're supposed to go home, like now, but could you just show us your darkroom really quick? Show us how you make pictures?"

That sounded like a fine idea to Rosemary.

And the kids had a blast. The three were crowded in the small space, and the girls seemed entranced with everything.

"The thing I'm confused about," Pepper said, "is why you're making your own photographs. I mean, couldn't you just get a digital camera? Or a phone where you could take pictures?"

"I could do both those things—and sometimes do," Rosemary explained. "But when I do these myself, then I own those photos. It's a legal thing. I'm responsible for the research and the work, so I wouldn't want anyone using my photos without my permission. It's like a protection."

"I get it." Lilly then had questions about the house— why it was so big and interesting, and was it really old, and how did she make the darkroom?

"The lodge has been in the MacKinnon family for generations—so lots of family members used it for summer getaways and vacations and holidays and just family gatherings. It was always kept pretty rustic, but when I knew I was going to be staying here for quite a while, I put in electricity and ran cable wires and all that." She motioned. "This used to be a utility room. It already had a sink and rough shelves. But when I set it up as a darkroom—well, one problem is that everything has to be put away perfectly—because once you've turned out the lights, you have to find what you need in the dark."

"So we can turn out the lights?" Lilly asked.

"Sure. But first let me show you what certain things are used for." The blackout shades had the obvious purpose. The extractor fan sucked out the chemical odors. She pointed out the safelight. And next to the old sink was a long "wet bench" made of something similar to Formica. "That's where the developing trays go—where you're developing the photos…and at the far end, there's a squeegee to remove excess water from the prints."

"This so beyond awesome," Lilly said.

"What's this stuff?" Pepper said as she pointed.

"All large bottles of solution are stored on the floor. Every single thing that's used in here has a place. And no matter how tired or busy I am, it all has to be put back in that place before I leave—or I'd never find it in the dark the next time."

"Well, that'd probably be too hard for me," Pepper admitted. "Dad says I shed stuff every place I walk, like a dog sheds fur."

"So what's that?" Lilly didn't want to listen to her sister. She wanted to hear Rosemary.

"Okay…on the other side of the room—and I know it's hard for the three of us to operate in this narrow space, but when I'm by myself, it's not so bad. So this is an enlarger. It does just what it sounds like. Makes the prints larger. It might make them blurrier, too—so you can't just ask it to enlarge something and then go take a nap. You have to watch the process."

"Rosemary?" Lilly again. "Could we do this with you sometime? If we didn't move and didn't get in your way and didn't do anything wrong? If we just watched?"

"Sure. If it's okay with your dad. And you guys are only going to be here for a week, aren't you?"

"We're not sure exactly. We think we're going home a day or two after Christmas, but Dad only promised that we'd be home by New Year's Eve, because we're sleeping over with a bunch of girls from school."

"We're going to stay up all night and have popcorn and stuff."

"Sounds like great fun." She heard a vague sound, turned her head, and abruptly realized that someone was knocking on the front door.

She hustled out, glanced out the peephole and felt her stomach jump five feet. She yanked open the door at the same time she looked at her watch.

"My God, Whit. I'm so sorry. I swear I didn't realize how much time had gone by."

"It's not a problem, except that when you gave me your cell number—"

She nodded. "I never heard it ring. I'm sorry. I think I left it on the fireplace mantel. And we were in the back of the house, the darkroom."

"Like I said, it's okay. But I did figure by now you'd need rescuing."

She did. Not from his girls. From him.

The minute he walked in the room, she suffered from a cavorting heartbeat and instant noodle knees, annoying her to no end. So he was a hunk. So he was so brawny he made her feel like a sweet little Southern belle. So he had the sexiest eyes this side of the Mississippi.

It was just attraction.

Last she knew, that problem was embarrassing but not fatal.

The kids leaped on him as if he'd been missing for six months. "Dad! Rosemary took us in the darkroom, and showed us all about the enlarger and the paper safe and the squeegee panels—"

"And where you keep the chemicals and the big extractor fan and solution and stuff—"

Since Whit was getting pulled inside, Rosemary interrupted with the obvious. "Would you like some tea or coffee? I've got both."

"Coffee, definitely, if it's not too much trouble."

By the time she brought two mugs back in, the girls had yelled for permission to play games on her iPad, and they'd taken root on the floor with couch pillows behind them. Whit, hands in his back pockets, was circling the corkboard display on the coffee table.

He smiled when she walked toward him, cocked his head toward the girls. "They've made themselves at home."

"It's the iPad. Not me."

"I don't think so. You keep gaining goddess status."

She laughed. "I'm not doing anything, honest."

"Maybe not, but we'll have to brainstorm some way to take you down a peg in their eyes. Otherwise, they're going to pester you nonstop."

He'd lowered his voice so the girls wouldn't hear. His whisper was just as evocative as his normal tenor.

"Well, if you think up something evil I could do, give a shout, would you?"

He chuckled. They shared a smile that made her feel like a lit sparkler in a dark room. But then he motioned toward her corkboard.

"The girls said you were doing a project with orchids."

She nodded. "The wild orchids in South Carolina— especially rare and endangered ones. Duke gave me a two-year grant, but I think I can finish the project sooner than that. When I came up here in June, that's all I did, traipse around the mountains, taking photographs and collecting specimens. So most of the gut research is done. I just have to put it all together, which is going to take a serious block of time." She knew she was babbling, but he honestly looked interested.

"Landscaping's my work."

"The twins said you owned a business."

He nodded. "I'm the family disgrace. I have three siblings, two lawyers and my sister is a CPA. I'm the only dirt bum. Love working with my hands. Love taking a piece of land—don't care whether it's small or big—and analyzing the soil, the shapes and contours, figuring out which plants and trees will thrive there, what will show it off. I have no idea where I picked up the addiction, but I sure have it hard-core."

"My parents are both surgeons, and they expected the three of us kids to follow in their footsteps…but at least I could share disgrace with one of my brothers. I went for botany, and Tucker has a retreat camp on Whisper Mountain here. Ike was the only brother who turned into a doctor, like we were all supposed to."

"Being a disgrace is tough."

"Well, I was a disgrace for more than one reason," she admitted, and then wanted to shoot herself. That wasn't information she meant to share with Whit—or anyone else, for that matter.

He didn't ask. He looked at her, as if waiting to hear the "other reason" she was a disgrace. But when she didn't say anything more, he turned his attention back to the corkboard of photographs.

"Are you only photographing them when they're in flower?" he asked.

"Good question. No. I marked the spot where I found each orchid—the location, the environment, the plants growing near them, tested the soil for acidity and all that. Then I went back every month to record that information all over again. Different predators showed up in different months. Different plants became dormant in different months. There were different insects, different temperatures, different rainfall."

"Man. I'd love to have done this kind of study. I don't know anything about orchids. But the how, why, when and where certain plants or grasses grow is of enormous interest to me."

"You didn't go for a botany degree...?"

"No, I went after a landscape architecture degree from Michigan State. It was a long way from home to go to college, but they had a great program for what I wanted. Never regretted it. But the study you're doing crosses paths with so much I'm interested in."

But he looked at her as if he were far more fascinated in her than her study. She couldn't remember the last time anyone wanted to hear what she thought, what she felt.

"Hey, Dad!" Pepper leaped up from the tablet and hurtled toward them at her usual speed—a full gallop. "Can we all stay and watch a movie if Rosemary says yes? There's one that starts in just a few minutes. We'll miss the beginning if we have to go home."

"I think our family's imposed on Rosemary enough for today."

"But *Dad*. It's *Princess Bride!* And it's on right now."

"You never have to see that one again. You know all the words. Hell. I know all the words. Please. Anything but that. Anything. We can even go home and talk about...clothes."

He herded them out, over a new round of protests and pleas and outright begging. Grabbed jackets. Found shoes. Listened to chatter.

Over their heads, before he whooshed them out the door, he looked at her. Really looked at her. As if they'd been connecting in a private way since the moment they met…the moment he walked in. Every moment they found themselves together.

She thought: he wanted to kiss her.

It was there. In his gaze. In how privately he looked at her, how silently he looked…worried. Worried but determined.

When she finally closed the door, the sudden silence in the cabin struck her again as unexpectedly lonely—when she'd been content living alone. Or she thought she'd been content.

She ambled through the living room, picking up mugs and glasses, doing little cleanups—and lecturing herself at the same time. She was imagining those "looks" from Whit. The guy was still in love with his wife, from everything the girls had said. He was still loving her, still mourning her, still grieving.

And she had no business volunteering for trouble, besides. She was still in deep emotional shock over George—the man everyone assumed she'd be thrilled to marry, thrilled to spend her life with. She hadn't discovered his turnip side until it was almost too late… which unfortunately said a whole lot about her lack of judgment in men.

She was afraid to trust her judgment again. Not because she was a sissy. Because she was smart.

She had to be smart. Her confidence had been crippled, not by George, but by misjudging a man she thought she loved. It was a mistake she couldn't risk making again.

Chapter Three

They'd been home a half hour. The girls were parked in front of *The Princess Bride,* mesmerized, as if they'd never seen the movie fifty times before. But Whit couldn't settle, couldn't shake an odd case of restlessness.

He prowled the rented house from room to room. The mountain cabin suited him far better than their home in Charleston—but Zoe loved the city side of life, so a city house was what she'd wanted.

He liked it here. The quiet. The clean air. The mists in the morning, the smell of pine, and the house itself had a dream of a layout. The great room had a massive corner fireplace, and the kitchen/dining area was all open. You could feed two or twenty in the same space. Glass doors everywhere led to a wraparound porch. The back door opened onto a practical mudroom and downstairs bath, and beyond that was a good size master bedroom.

The upstairs was a simple open loft—a bedroom and den type of area—the girls had squealed nonstop when they first saw it, thought it was "beyond awesome" to have a whole floor to themselves. He thought it was equally "awesome" that they were always safely within his sight.

When he'd prowled the house enough, he settled with a mug of cider in the great room—as far away from *The Princess Bride* movie as he could get—and accidently found himself staring out the glass doors to the west. More precisely, he wasn't staring out, but staring up.

He couldn't see the MacKinnon lodge through the thick forest, but without those trees, he suspected he'd easily be able to locate Rosemary's place, maybe even see her, if she were outside on her front deck.

Mentally he could still picture her long legs, the careless, easy way she wore clothes. Her hair was short, blond as sunshine, always looking finger-brushed, framing her delicate face so naturally. The way her sun-blushed skin set off added to her looks being striking, interesting.

More than interesting. He hadn't felt his hormones kick like this in a long, long time.

There was a reason—there had to be a reason—why a smart, delectably attractive and downright interesting woman was living alone. It gnawed at him to think of her being alone, especially during the holidays. It wasn't as if there were close neighbors or friends who could easily stop over for a visit. Whit understood that she'd won that academic grant, that she loved the study, that whole business.

But that still didn't explain her holing up alone for the holidays.

And it didn't begin to explain the sadness in her blue blue eyes.

Abruptly he heard the tune on his cell phone, flipped it open and heard the country drawl of Samson, one of his truck drivers. No emergency, Sam just wanted to relay that he was headed to Savannah for his Christmas family gathering, and he hoped Whit and the girls would have a good holiday.

The conversation lifted his spirits. His employees had been together for years now, except for a few extra college kids he'd hired over the summer. They'd turned into a team, the kind who shared good times and bad, who attended each other's christenings and graduations.

Whit didn't know what that really meant until Zoe died, and the crew hung closer to him than sticky glue. Someone called every day; someone else brought food; and all of them offered help with whatever needed doing—either for Whit or for the girls. It taught him forever that "family" could mean a lot of things, and wasn't always defined by blood kin.

When he finished the call, he almost put down the phone...but instead flipped it open again. Rosemary's number was already in his phone's memory, from their first call. It only took one impulsive, brainless moment to dial it.

Her line was busy.

So, he thought, she did have someone to talk to.

He couldn't call again for a couple hours, because the

movie ended and the girls immediately claimed starvation. The vote for dinner was a made-from-scratch pizza—one of the few things he could do well in the kitchen. It just always seemed to require every dish and every counter to put it together.

The girls helped clean up. Some. Predictably, though, they scattered faster than dust in the wind when he turned on the news.

Once they ran upstairs, he tried calling Rosemary again.

For the second time, her line was busy. So she either had another person to talk with, or she'd talked for three solid hours to her first caller. The former seemed more likely, but as the girls came back down to con Whit into an old fashioned game of Clue, he got the niggling idea that possibly she was in trouble. Maybe she hadn't been talking. Maybe her phone wasn't working, because for a hermit to be occupied with two calls seemed odd. A puzzle piece that didn't fit.

If that thinking was flimsy, he figured out the obvious. He wanted to talk with her. Any excuse he could conjure up was good enough.

He checked on the girls, found them in their Christmas pj's, lying on their tummies reading. He stole a good-night kiss from each, then took his cell phone into his room downstairs.

He kicked off his shoes, flipped off the light and sank into the recliner facing the west glass doors. The master bedroom suited him like a good pair of gloves. Nothing fancy, just a giant bed with a serious mattress and a warm, dark pine comforter. The best part was the view. The glass doors looked straight up the mountainside. A few nights before there'd been a full moon. He'd been close enough to touch it.

Okay, so maybe not that close. But he'd moved the recliner to the window that night, and that's where he'd spent the past few evenings since, a short brandy in his hand, the lights off, to just inhale the mountain, the air, the peace.

When he dialed Rosemary's number this time, she answered. "Whit? Trouble at your house?"

She sounded breathless, animated. "No trouble. Did I catch you in the middle of something?"

"Yeah. Stargazing."

She didn't chuckle but he could hear the smile in her voice.

"I was doing that here, too. I just shut off the lights. I can't get over how many stars I can see from this altitude."

"It's the mountain. You know the mountain's full of magic, don't you?"

"Oh, yeah. I'm a real believer in magic," he said drily.

Again, he could hear the smile in her voice. "Whisper Mountain has a legend. The 'whisper' business is supposed to be real. Except that only true lovers can hear the mountain whisper. It's a sign."

"You mean like a stop sign or a construction warning sign?"

"No, you lunkhead. It's a *magic* sign."

"Did you just call me a lunkhead?"

"No, of course not. That was the other woman on the phone. Not me. I don't even know what a lunkhead is. I never heard the word before."

"Well, would you put Rosemary back on the line?"

"Can't. She's in the bathtub shaving her legs. Took a glass of wine and a candle with her, so I doubt she's coming out soon."

"Is it me, or is this conversation coming out of never-never land?"

"What do you expect? You're living with two pre-teen girls and I live alone. After nine o'clock, I don't think it's reasonable to expect rational conversation."

"Well, I swear, there was a rational reason why I called you. But now—"

"You can't remember it? You're feeling a little discombobulated?"

"That wasn't the first word that came to mind. But once you said it, yes."

"Well, I can pretty well guess why you called. I thought a little estrogen-spiced conversation might scare you off, but so far it doesn't seem to be working.... So yeah, I'll go Christmas tree hunting with you three tomorrow."

For a moment he was speechless. "How did you know I was calling for that?"

"Because your girls brought it up about fifty times—that you were going to find your own tree, bring it home, do the really traditional holiday things. And after spending a couple hours with the twins, I figured you'd started to realize that an entire week alone with two girls that age could strain your sanity—no matter how much you love your daughters. And they're adorable. Anyway..."

Sitting on a chair, Whit couldn't figure out why he felt so dizzy. "Anyway?"

"Anyway, the last thing I want to do is intrude on

your family time. I'm not an Aunt Matilda, who you have to invite for holiday stuff because she's alone. I'm fine here. One hundred percent fine. Two hundred percent fine even. Just because the girls were bubbling with invitations, you're talking to me now, and I promise, I didn't take them seriously."

"I'm going to have to hang up pretty soon, because you're starting to make sense and that's scaring me." Then he added quickly, "But tomorrow, we figured on taking the Gator, doing a search-and-cut for Christmas trees. I figure around ten in the morning, if it's not raining? And that's a 'please come' from all three of us, not just Pepper and Lilly."

"All right, all right! I'll come. I can't resist the three of you! But...I'm going back to my stargazing now. If I quit doing this, I'll have run out of excuses for not working. I've got hours of soil samples I have to analyze, so you can't imagine how happy I am that you called. I got to postpone work even longer."

She rang off before he could reply. His first impulse was to shake his head, hard, see if he could get some airflow back to his brain.

But his second impulse was to just laugh. Hell. He could feel a wreath of a smile on his face. The call had been completely off the wall and nonsensical...but he couldn't remember laughing in a long time. Even smiling some days was a job.

Since Zoe died, he'd almost forgotten that he used to be a happy-go-lucky kind of guy. Laughter used to come to him easy as sunshine. As a kid, he'd been prone to a little trouble, couldn't shake the mischief gene, but marriage had shaped him up. The twins came six months after the wedding. Neither he nor Zoe was ready for marriage, but she'd had an early ultrasound, so they knew about the twins.

There was no way they could give up two. Or raise two without each other. He was a little mad at first. So was she. Before the babies, they'd both realized that their love affair was more of a lust affair, and the marriage was on precarious ground. But then the girls came. Whit still remembered the first time he'd held his newborn daughters.

He'd been a goner. That fast. That completely. He never knew he had a daddy streak, much less that he would go head over heels hopeless for the squirts. Neither slept at night. They cried in unison, never a little whine, always screams loud enough to wake the dead. If one didn't have a messy diaper, the other did.

The babies had not only terrorized him; they'd terrified him. In spite of that—in spite of everything—the bond kept growing. He'd have given his life for them. Without a qualm.

Abruptly he heard a noisy attack of giggles coming from the loft. Since they were obviously still awake, he ambled toward the stairs. They were going to love the news that Rosemary was joining them tomorrow.

Still, just from talking on the phone with her, he felt a goofball smile glued on his face. She had that kind of dry humor, the way she talked total nonsense in such a serious tone.

Whit might have killed for his daughters…but it had been a long time since he'd felt anything to live for, beyond the girls. He couldn't remember smiling…just for himself. He couldn't remember the last time he'd felt lighthearted—and he had no idea why or how Rosemary had evoked those forgotten emotions in him.

But he was glad he was seeing her tomorrow.

After that…well, he'd just have to see.

Rosemary was trying to pull on thick wool socks and hold the cell phone at the same time. It was not an easy balance act.

"I swear, Tucker, no one could be more of a pain than a brother—unless both you and Ike were calling me at the same time. Just tell me how the new wife is. And how her pregnancy is going. And how the boys are—"

"Everybody's fine." Tucker would do anything for her and she knew it, but her oldest brother was more stubborn than a mule. "But I still want you to agree to have Christmas with us. You don't have to see Mom and Dad. You could just—"

"Tucker! I told you and Ike both that I can't do that. I don't want to hurt the parents. I just can't handle one more conversation about why I canceled the wedding, what George must have done, what I must have done, how I could fix it all if I just called him, etcetera, etcetera, etcetera. I've heard it too many times. I don't *want* to miss any of you at Christmas. Even though you're both total pains, I love you. And your families. I even love Pansy, that damned bloodhound Ike made me babysit for."

"But—"

She wasn't about to hear him repeat his argument. "But nothing. I told Mom and Dad that I had to work. If anyone in the universe could understand that, it's them.

And it's not like I won't catch up with all of you. I already sent heaps of presents to the kids—"

Tucker, of course, interrupted with different persuasive arguments. Being relentless wasn't totally his fault. Growing up with absentee parents—and their parents were such terrific surgeons that they were always on call—Tucker had taken on the role of Dad. Being the only girl, Rosemary had tried to play the role of Mom, but since she was the youngest, all she could really do was hand out suckers when the boys were sick. The point, though, was that Tucker thought she needed a caretaker.

Which she did. But not a brother or a dad or a lover. Not a man at all.

She needed to be her own caretaker.

Still, she listened to her older brother's rant—or mostly listened—as she walked to the closet to retrieve her serious jacket, then ambled over to the front window. Whit and the girls would be here any moment. It was after ten now.

Outside, there was brilliant—but misleading sunshine. She'd hiked before dawn, almost froze to death. The sleet had started in the middle of the night and stopped before daybreak. But there were still tears dripping from every pine branch, crystal ice on every puddle. She needed wool mittens, and wasn't sure where she'd seen them last.

"Rosemary...Ike said something about a guy there."

"Oh, for heaven's sake. You two are like mother hens, I swear."

"Well, you're all alone up there. And if it were me

all alone, you'd be checking out how I was doing. No difference."

"Of course it's different. You think because I'm a girl, I'm less capable. Who whipped you at poker last time, huh? Who beat you in the kayak race last fall? Who—?"

"Those were technicalities. I'm the big brother, so I had to let you win."

She made a rude sound into the phone, making him sputter with laughter. Her eyes were still peeled on the gravel road, though. It didn't matter if Whit was late or early. They were on vacation during the holiday week, so it's not as if they were compelled to stick to a schedule.

Tucker eventually circled back to his nosy grilling. "About this guy."

"I only mentioned my temporary neighbor to Ike because he was bugging me about being alone—he wasn't as awful as you, but close. Anyway, that's why I mentioned that a very, very nice guy rented a house for the holidays. He has twin daughters, around eleven—"

"Very nice, huh?"

"If you won't interrupt, I'll fill in the blanks. He's a widower. Major car accident a year ago, and his wife was killed. So he came up here with his girls to have a private Christmas away from the memories."

"Okay."

"Get that tone out of your voice, Tucker, or I swear, I'll sock you when I see you next, in front of the boys."

"I was just asking...." Tucker had that innocent tone down by rote.

"He's grieving. Hard. For his wife. It's pretty obvious he's still in love with her and can't get over the loss. The girls accidently came across to the lodge. That's the only reason we met."

"Okay, that sounds..." Her brother searched for a word. "Nice."

"It is nice. He's nice. The girls are nice. But the only thing on their minds is the loss they suffered last year. It's a sad time of year for them. That's all."

"Okay, okay, I got it. Sheesh." Tucker hesitated. "All the same, if you wanted, I could run a background check on him—"

She hung up. Sometimes that's all you could do with brothers. It was something in the male sibling gene. When they got a bone between their teeth, they all turned into Neanderthals.

And just then, she saw a sturdy SUV winding up the driveway. The girls were here.

And so was their dad.

Whit couldn't take his eyes off her. She bounced out of the house like a kid, a stocking hat yanked over her head, wearing old hiking boots and skinny jeans and a Christmas red parka.

"Hey, Rosemary!" the girls called out.

"Hey right back! Does everybody have mittens?" She opened the passenger door, but didn't climb in yet. The girls had automatically taken the backseat, assuming anyone of adult age would want to sit up front. Which pretty much meant they intended to lean over Rosemary's seat the whole time.

"Who'd have guessed it would be this cold?" Rosemary said, and kept talking. "I figured you'd change

your mind about the Gator and bring a bigger car. Don't
know how we'd carry trees and the four of us together,
otherwise. Anyway, I have spare mittens and hats and
gloves in the lodge, if anyone needs stuff like that.
Nothing pretty. Just warm."

Lilly said, "I brought gloves, but Pepper didn't. She
always says she doesn't need them, but two seconds
later, she's freezing to death."

"You *lie*," Pepper shot back.

"I'm not lying, I'm—"

Rosemary shot Whit a wink, then just hustled back
in the house and came out moments later with a bag
full of cold-weather gear. She jumped back in, belted
up, handed the bag to the girls and that was it. The girls
pulled out gloves and mufflers and leg warmers and
hats. Just like that, the three females all started talking
at the same time, nonstop. Rosemary carried on two if
not three conversations simultaneously…as if she'd always been with them, always been part of the family.

Part of his life.

Maybe she was primarily talking to the girls about
mittens versus gloves, who knitted what, what colors
looked good with their hair, how both of them desperately needed new jeans, and a bunch about movies he'd
never heard of—except, of course *The Princess Bride*.

Somehow, though, she managed to answer a question from him about the lodge in the middle of all that.

"I'm not sure how big the lodge is—I think three
thousand square feet or so? My great grandparents
built it originally…when families tended to be bigger,
and cousins and uncles and spare relatives all wanted

a place to get together, so they needed a monster-size place like that..."

Whit wasn't sure where he was going. The gravel road wrapped around the mountaintop like a drunken ribbon, dipping here, climbing there, branches sometimes scraping the sides of the SUV. There was a lot of virgin forest this high, which meant the trees were tall and huge, nothing appropriate for a Christmas tree. Still, trees fell and new growth always emerged. He wasn't looking for perfect trees, just two that had little chance of making it on their own.

In the meantime, she answered another question. "It was kept primitive for a lot of years—no electricity, no hot water. But my brothers and I got into it last year. To start with, we built a solar oven..."

"You're kidding."

"Well, I built most of it. Of course that's not what they'd tell you, because they can't stand it that I'm pretty good with power tools. Tucker put in an on demand water heater, and Ike built the current kitchen table from reclaimed heart pine. Our grandparents never had a generator. I bought that. Once I planned to stay here for quite a while, I needed a way to store food at safe temperatures—not counting needing computers and printers and a phone. Living alone never bothered me, but I definitely needed a way to work and a way to communicate with the outside world."

No matter what he asked, she answered...but that turned into a tit for tat. She had questions of her own. Not over personal subjects, just friendly queries about their lives. Yes, they lived in Charleston, partly because Zoe adamantly loved city life—and both of them wanted an area with great schools.

Pepper piped in, just to make sure they knew she was listening in. "Aw, come on, Dad. You know we think school is b-o-r-i-n-g. We could move somewhere else if we wanted to. It's not like there aren't schools all over the place."

The girls listened just as intently when Rosemary asked him about his landscaping business. He had a handful of regular employees and hired temporary help during the planting and growing seasons. "I really like doing larger scapes, like for businesses, community centers, university planning...but overall, I've always loved working with dirt, more than sitting at a desk chair. I'm just lucky to have found something I love, with a lot of variety and something new every day."

"There's nothing like it, is there?" she mused. "Doing work you love? I went into botany for the same reasons—I wanted to be outside more than inside, didn't want to sit in a fancy office all day."

"Mom used to say that nobody could get dirtier than Dad. She used to say that he walked outside and dirt flew on him." Lilly provided this information.

Pepper added detail. "My mom wanted white carpeting in the living room. But then she said better not, because Dad would never be allowed in there."

"But then she said it didn't make any difference, because Dad would rather have a beer at the kitchen table than wine at a party."

He felt Rosemary glance at him. The girls could never be trusted to not talk a stranger's ear off, and they had no sense of boundaries for what was off-limits. But their mom was okay to talk about. And the white carpet conversation was nothing weird. Still, he felt her gaze on him, a question in the sudden silence that she never asked.

That was okay. He finally found a good spot to stop, where a range of young trees struggled for growth on the shade side of the mountain. As far as Whit was concerned, he'd found the site just in time.

He couldn't remember being more sexually conscious of a woman in a long time. She was so natural. Earthy. Easy. No airs, no high-heel attitudes. Just pure female.

She flooded the front seat with estrogen, something tantalizing, alluring.

So it was a damned good thing he could open the door, pop out and get some bracing cold air in his lungs.

"Okay, here's the deal, ladies. We don't want a perfect tree. We want a hopelessly ugly tree. A tree so weirdly shaped that it probably doesn't have much chance to survive. That way we're cutting down a tree that needs a future in our Christmas, because that's probably the best future it's got. And small." He motioned to his shoulder. "No taller than that. And we need two, one for our place, and one for Rosemary's."

"Honest, guys, I'm happy to do this with you, but I don't really need a tree," Rosemary said.

"Yes she does, Dad. She doesn't have any lights or wreaths or anything at her place. She *really* needs a tree. Even more than us."

"Lilly has spoken," he said apologetically. "Sorry, but you're getting a tree."

The three peeled out of the car before he even had

his door closed. The first tree took the longest to find. It had to be suitably ugly, suitably small. Crooked, not straight, thin in the branches, pitiful. Since Lilly loved every tree, it was tough to make a decision—it was *always* tough for the girls to agree on anything, and when they finally did, the three females deserted him. While he took the tools from the back of the SUV, they went searching for the second tree.

It didn't take long, to cut down the scrawny trunk, wrap a tarp to secure the branches and haul it to the top of the car. By the time he turned around, the girls were nowhere.

They had to be close. He'd heard them all chattering moments before—Lilly saying, "Darn it, it's starting to rain."

And Rosemary correcting her, "Look up, hon. That's not rain—it's white stuff coming down. It's snow."

And then Pepper aiming for high volume, "*Snow!* I haven't seen *snow* in my whole life!"

Truthfully, the sky was barely spitting white than offering a true snowfall, but he had to grin, too, at the soft splash of white crystals drifting down. He ambled in the direction of the last conversation he'd heard. They couldn't have gone far, and he wasn't remotely worried. If there'd been a bear in a five-mile vicinity, it would have to be an awfully dumb bear. The three thrashing and crashing through the woods could have scared an ogre or worse.

Still, when he called out, "Rosemary? Lilly and Pep?" there was no answer.

Seconds later, he found out why. He wove around a cluster of pines, and found a barren patch...where all three were lying on the ground next to each other. All three had closed their eyes. All three had stuck out their tongues.

They were all trying to catch the taste of a snow-flake.

Damned, if his heart didn't suddenly start squeezing tight in his chest.

Zoe, their mom, would never have gone for the tree adventure. She'd have been waiting at home, with the prized ornaments and lights, and the artificial tree she loved so much. Zoe would never have laid on the ground in the woods. She'd never have closed her eyes and stuck out her tongue

Whit tried to take his eyes off her. Not his daughters. Just Rosemary. The joy on her face, the easy fun in her grin, the way his daughters were bookends to her. So she was a little taller. But her stocking cap and mittens looked as silly as theirs, as fun

Her lips had a wet cherry hue…and her cheeks already had sharp blush from the wind.

He looked and kept looking and couldn't explain it. But watching her try to taste snowflakes caused an avalanche of sudden emotion he'd never expected.

He could fall in love with this woman. Maybe he was already half falling. And he hadn't even kissed her…. But then, he'd never expected to fall in love with anyone ever again.

Chapter Four

Rosemary had to laugh. The girls poured through her front door and threw themselves on the old leather couches as if they couldn't make it another inch.

"I've never been so tired in my whole life!" Pepper said.

"You're such a wuss. There's nothing to be tired about. But I sure am hungry. *Really* hungry, Rosemary—"

"Well, me, too," she admitted as she hooked her red parka on the hall tree and heeled off her boots. "I wasn't exactly planning for company, but I've got a full freezer. The fastest would probably be chili. I made a batch weeks ago, and froze half of it."

"Is it really spicy?" Lilly asked.

"Afraid not. I didn't have any hot peppers to put in, and I pretty much tend to make it mild anyway."

"*Good.* That sounds *great,* then."

"You don't have to feed us." Whit came in last, because he was carrying the tree. Thankfully he'd brought a bucket to put it in, because Rosemary was pretty sure she'd never find the one they'd used at the lodge. The MacKinnons had spent a zillion holidays here. Both the attic and one whole closet held decorations and tableware for Christmas, but she had no memory of seeing a tree stand.

"It's no trouble," she assured Whit. "I just have to thaw and heat it. Won't take more than a few minutes."

She was humming as she aimed for the kitchen. She'd always loved the old room, with its wide beams and plank floor and rustic wood cupboard—the subzero freezer blended in just fine, as far as she was concerned. Only took two shakes to take the container from the freezer, pop it in the microwave and start herding bowls together from the far cupboard.

As she pulled out the silverware drawer, she was still humming, half dancing around the room. Checked the chili in the microwave, gave it a serious stir, punched it on again. Darned if she could remember the song in her head, but she couldn't stop humming. She even knew why.

She was downright *happy*. What a great morning. All four of them had been laughing and having fun. Maybe the three Cochrans could have done the same thing without her—but she'd loved being part of their group. The girls ganged up with her against Whit, the poor lone guy against the assault of estrogen. Lilly had laughed once so much she had to hold her stomach.

Whit had to think she had some dingbat genes when he caught the three lying on their backs on the cold ground—but what difference did it make?

She wasn't trying to lure him. She was just trying to help the three have a happy, carefree holiday, where grieving for their mom was eased a bit.

"On the table," she yelled out a few minutes later, and the three hurtled in the room at Olympic speed. They were hungry. "It's not fancy," she began. "And I'm not used to cooking much—"

Whit squeezed her shoulder. Her head shot up—but he wasn't looking at her, only aiming past her in the crowded space between wall and chairs. Still, she felt the imprint of his big hand, the gentleness of it, the sudden unexpected scissor-sharp awareness.

Immediately she put that thought to bed. There was no reason on earth to think his touch had been anything but kindness or friendly affection or something like that. And the girls dug into the chili as if they hadn't eaten in a year.

"Like pigs at a trough." Whit sighed, which earned him a chorus of *"Dad!"* from his offended daughters.

She chuckled. "If anyone's still hungry after this, I have a few—*very* few—brownies that some fabulous bakers happened to leave me...."

"She's talking about us, Dad."

"No kidding?"

Once they'd leveled all the food in sight, they clustered back in the living room to argue about where she "needed" the tree. Lilly wanted it by the fireplace; Pepper wanted it in front of a window. Whit didn't care, as long as he didn't have to keep carting it around from place to place while the girls made up their minds.

Eventually, it seemed to occur to the twins that possibly Rosemary should get a vote. She struggled to find a solution that wouldn't hurt either girl's feelings. "Well," she said slowly, "I like both your ideas better...but I feel kind of stuck, choosing the far corner by the front window. That place is the traditional tree spot in the MacKinnon family for as far back as I can remember."

"It's totally okay," Lilly immediately assured her. Not for the first time, she noted that Lilly was always the one to watch out for other's feelings, even coming to stand by her in support.

So after much groaning and grunting and pine needles all over the floor, Whit finished securing the tree in the holder, and the girls asked for a white sheet to drape around the bottom. Then they all stood back.

"So what do you think?" Whit asked in a gravely serious voice.

"Words almost fail me," Rosemary said. "But the first ones that come to mind are pitiful. Above and beyond any definition of ugly that I can think of. The poorest excuse for a Christmas tree I've ever seen in my life."

"Don't hold back now," Whit encouraged her.

The tree had branches at the top, but then a half foot where the trunk had either lost its branches or never had any. The bottom quarter was straggly, some branches sticking out like lone strangers. The trunk was not just lopsided, but crooked.

The girls agreed on the awfulness. But Rosemary had to pipe up again. "If ever a tree needed loving, it's this one."

"And besides, Rosemary, it looks half dead and all goofed up already. So it wasn't going to live long." Lilly was obviously serious about trees.

"So we didn't hurt anything but taking it out of the forest."

"And it smells like a good tree."

It smelled like Christmas, Rosemary thought—a smell she'd never thought she'd have a chance to love this year. She felt Whit's eyes on her face...half turned to see a private smile aimed her way. "I'll never look for a perfect tree again," she announced. "Not once I can see how right a tree like this belongs here."

"Ours is even uglier, I'm guessing," Pepper said. "We won't know until we get it home."

"Okay," Whit said. "Let's clean up here and then get out of Rosemary's hair. We've got messes to make at our house."

For the three, she doled out brooms and a container for trash, but aimed for the kitchen herself. She'd rather be cleaning up with the crew, but facing dishes with dried-on chili later just wasn't appealing. Besides, it only took a few minutes to collect the dishes, feed them to the dishwasher and wipe down the counters. From the living room, she heard the front door open and close— Whit taking out tools and debris, she suspected—and the usual sound of the girls' chatter.

She was just hanging up a dish towel when she realized there was suddenly silence coming from the great room. She hung the towel, squeezed a dollop of almond hand cream from the dispenser, and glanced around the corner.

Whit had not only cleaned up the tree mess, but brought in kindling and firewood and started a fire. He was an artist at it, she noticed. The crisscross bed was meticulously created, the poke of kindling spearing through the dry brush, the bed of branches fitting like Lincoln Logs. Yellow wicks of fire had already caught and were snipping and scissoring around the kindling.

Bemused, she looked away from the dancing flames...and immediately spotted the girls. They'd crashed like puppies. Lilly had curled at one end of the biggest leather couch and tugged a throw over herself. Pepper had done a total sprawl, stealing three quarters of the couch space, with an arm flung here, a leg flung there, a what-you-see-is-what-you-get kind of deep, abandoned sleep.

She glanced around, but didn't immediately see Whit. Before going to look for him, she scouted around for a second throw blanket, found one at the top of the hall closet, and quietly draped it over Pepper.

After that, she tiptoed around, finally noticed his silhouette on the back porch. She grabbed a jacket to pull over her shoulders and stepped outside.

He turned, with a smile for her.

"I was just about to grab the girls and take off when I saw they'd fallen asleep on the couch. But you're busy. And I can—"

"They're fine, Whit. I had to crack up a little. They're so like little kids, run a hundred miles an hour nonstop...but when they're tired, they drop like stones."

"They had a terrific time."

"Me, too. Good to have noise and laughter and commotion in the lodge again." She took a couple steps so she could stand next to him, looking out where he was. The promise of snow had disappeared, but there were still pockets of white, confectioner's sugar in the tucks of trees, hidden in branches, clustered on rocks.

A stream wound a silver ribbon, not big, just enough to make a clean, rushing sound over rocks and stony banks.

It was cold enough to freeze her nose, but she didn't move. Standing next to him, she was aware of his greater height, the brawn of him compared to her lean frame.

"This place is magic," he said quietly. "I'd have a hard time leaving it, if I lived here."

"Yeah. I love it, too. For a few years, no one really used it…but when my grandparents were alive, we often had holidays here. I remember so many times, cousins and extra kids running around having a ball. So much space. So many places to explore and enjoy."

"Sounds as if you had an idyllic childhood."

"It mostly was. I think I mentioned before that both my parents are surgeons, part of the Greenville Health System. We had a lot of birthdays and holidays interrupted by emergency calls—but my two brothers spoiled me beyond belief. Still do." She tugged her jacket tighter, not wanting to go inside, just starting to freeze. "I still remember one of the first guys I went out with. My brothers never let him through the interview process—*their* interview process. The guy had this little red sports car. Just adorable. I could have killed Tucker and Ike both."

He chuckled. "Good memories."

"In every way. Both brothers got married just this year. I'd like to think that because of superb sisterly coaching, that they knew how to pick outstanding women. Or I guess it's possible that they just lucked out."

He chuckled again, then gave her a thoughtful look. "But you're alone here over the holidays."

She took a breath. It didn't sound as if he were prying, more like he was trying to make sense out of it, put the pieces together of other things she'd told him.

"It's not as if I wanted to be alone exactly. It just seemed the only choice I had, this particular year." She hesitated. "For my parents, I always tried to be the little girl who wasn't demanding, who didn't want to cause them any worry. And for my brothers, they've always been so darned good to me, that I just didn't want to disappoint them."

"Hard to imagine you could."

"Thanks. But I definitely did. I was engaged last year, was supposed to be married in June. I broke it off. Just weeks before the wedding."

"Ouch. That couldn't have been a happy deal."

"About as painful as you could get. But there were reasons why I couldn't explain the situation completely to family. I wasn't trying to duck the problem. I just felt I didn't have a choice. So I pretended as if I had way too much work to do—which is partly the truth, if I want to finish this grant earlier than expected. And the other part of the truth is that especially my parents understand heavy work schedules."

He glanced out toward the stream again, as if trying to figure out what to say. "So this grant...you're aiming for a Ph.D.?"

"It sure seems that way. Truthfully I'd never planned on getting a Ph.D., and I liked the work I was doing before. But I had to do *something* after the breakup, and I knew a certain prof at Duke. He knew about some open grants, mentioned the two-year project on the wild orchids. It just hit me at the perfect time. The money wasn't that great, but good enough to live on. And I loved the project, so it all worked out."

Neither said anything after that. She hadn't spoken to anyone but her ex-fiancé. It wasn't as if she'd spilled the mortifying part of the story…but it felt unexpectedly good just to tell someone, to feel Whit had somehow become enough of a friend to trust him with some personal things about her life.

It was just…suddenly she realized they were standing extremely close.

She assumed they were standing that close so they could talk in whispers, not wanting the girls to hear them.

She assumed that he was looking at her just as a natural way of responding to the conversation.

Only suddenly she couldn't remember the conversation. And he wasn't looking at her like a new acquaintance or a neighbor or the father of two girls. He was looking at her as if she was the only woman in the universe—at least his universe.

She backed up a step. Or half a step. Behind her seemed to be a log wall, nowhere else to go, no place else to move. Of course she had the choice to say something intelligent, like what on earth do you think you're doing?

Only he was already leaning in to her by then. She saw his eyes. Deep blue and getting bluer.

Some instinct sent adrenaline spearing through her pulse. She couldn't imagine why. She'd grown up with brothers, been around men all her life. Of course,

George had demolished her confidence, sabotaged her judgment...but even so, she was absolutely positive she had no reason to fear Whit.

But there it was. That whistle and heat of danger, of warning, that suddenly made her heart pound. And all he was doing was leaning down, his eyes open, on hers, watching, waiting.

When his mouth connected with hers, a switch flipped on in her head, forcing her to close her eyes, to sink back, to feel her bones turn liquid.

It was just a kiss. She told herself that once. Twice. Three times. She even believed it.

Only there was something in Whit. Something that was different to her, for her. Her hormones suddenly jolted awake.

His lips tasted like something...alluring, intoxicating. The kiss started with no pressure, then sneaked down to another level, an earthier level, an exploring secrets, just-let-go level.

His mouth lifted. She opened her eyes, saw his expression, surprise, interest. He could have stopped then, but no, he came back for another kiss, this one involving sound and pressure. He cocked his leg, needing support to lean down to her level for so long...but then she was almost on tiptoe by then; he was damned tall...and she had to wind her arms around his neck. Had to. Because otherwise she would have fallen.

Her fingertips sieved into his hair, then stroked the long muscles of his neck. He was so strong, his upper arms solid as a tree trunk. She'd always been strong and fit in her own right, but Whit was like an oak...where lately she'd felt as fragile as a reed.

She murmured, "The girls."

Mentioning his daughters had no effect. Possibly if the girls showed up, appeared in the doorway, they'd both get a brain. Only the girls were nowhere in sight, and Whit was still kissing her.

He deserted her mouth, sank lips into her throat, her neck. His eyes were closed, as if the only thing in his sphere of attention was her. When he shifted, she felt his arousal graze against her, reminding her that this was no boy playing with flirtation and desire, but a grown man.

Definitely a grown man.

With a grown man's needs…and a grown man's earthy hunger. An appetite he seemed to definitely have….

For her.

"Whit…"

She was pretty sure he heard her this time. A hundred percent certain he'd stop if she asked him. Only he seemed to hear invitation in her voice instead of the warning she had in mind.

"Whit," she tried again, and tipped her head to enable a kiss that started from her. Hell's bells, if he was that determined to get into trouble, she might as well dive in deep water, too.

No one had wanted her—certainly not her ex-fiancé—the way Whit seemed to. She'd always picked good men, believed she had reasonably good taste in men. Only the good guys she'd picked in the past seemed to find her amazingly replaceable.

Not that she was pretending Whit could have serious feelings for her. They'd just met, for heaven's sake.

She'd always been a practical realist. She never thought for an instant that Whit was thinking about her in any kind of serious way. This was just a kiss.

A kiss that kept coming.

That kept building.

A kiss that wouldn't stop, wouldn't quell, wouldn't behave.

Suddenly he lifted his head. His mouth was still damp, half open, and his hair was rumpled—from her hands—his face flushed. But a frown pinched his forehead. The first frown she'd seen on his face.

"Hey," he said.

"That's exactly what I was thinking. Hey."

The frown eased. His gaze never left hers. He searched her face—owned her wet mouth, owned the shaky silvery look in her eyes. "I just wasn't expecting…"

"Neither was I," she said swiftly. "You don't have to tell me. This just isn't a good idea."

Now he tilted his head, as if confused. "It's not a good idea because?"

Her voice was soft, but she said the obvious. "Because your girls are grieving for their mom. Because you are. Because I wouldn't want any of you worried even for a second that I thought I could take her place. Especially on a holiday, when she must be especially on all your minds."

Again he looked perplexed. Then he brushed a rough thumb against the line of her jaw. "Rosemary. I was kissing you, not the wife I lost. I was thinking about you. Not her."

She smiled. It was a nice thing to say. She didn't believe him for a minute, but the kindness in his nature touched her, warmed her.

A loud shriek echoed from the living room, followed by a second one. As far as she could tell, the girls got along like two peas in a pod...until they didn't.

She cast a rueful glance at Whit, and if her heart hadn't been so scrambled, she might have chuckled. He was tucking in his shirt as fast as she was grabbing her jacket from the ground, straightening her sweater, raking a hand through his hair the same way she was trying to smooth down hers. He shot her a quick, stolen smile—how could she help not smiling back?

But then...that was it. One of the girls woke up, then the other; Whit gathered up their gear and in a matter of minutes, they were gone.

She rubbed her arms uneasily. The silence hit her the same way as when they'd left last time. She knew she was independent, comfortable alone...but now the quiet itched on her heart like a mosquito bite. The verdant Christmas tree filled her vision, and the scent of fresh pine brought back every loving Christmas memory she'd ever had.

She wanted family, a yearning so sharp it hurt sometimes. She didn't want a marriage like her parents had—where work dominated both their lives more than family. But she and her brothers loved time together. They laughed, teased, supported and fought together. But more than anything they did, Rosemary felt safe with her brothers the way she'd never felt with outsiders.

That was what she wanted. A man she could be herself with. A man who wanted the kind of family she did—not perfect, not storybook, not pretend—but the real kind of family where you could let down your hair and always know, always, that they'd stand up for you.

From everything she'd seen so far…Whit was that kind of man. He couldn't be the kind of father she'd seen if he weren't that kind of man. But he must have deeply, hugely loved his wife to be that kind of man as well—and a strange woman in the picture of this specific Christmas was just totally wrong.

So there'd been a kiss.

Okay, more than a kiss.

Okay, a whole lot more than a kiss—at least for her. But she could put it out of her mind. For their sakes.

Whit was on his second mug of coffee when the girls woke up. Typical of a Saturday morning, Lilly sprang awake at gallop speed to greet the day…where Pepper slouched into the kitchen with a yawn and a scowl, daring anyone to speak to her before she'd had her favorite cereal and a banana.

He'd woken before dawn, found himself staring out the window, waiting for the sun to come up, replaying that embrace with Rosemary over and over in his mind.

Maybe he'd liked her on sight, but he'd never expected Armageddon or the Clash of Titans emanating from a first kiss. But it had. It troubled him that Rosemary clearly believed he was pining for his wife…the truth was more complex than that, and probably not a truth that he knew how to share. He'd never tried putting words to his feelings. Certainly not with a woman he barely knew.

But it festered more why she was living like a hermit, what exactly her damn fool fiancé had done that was so profound she'd shut herself away. He assumed the jerk had cheated on her...wasn't that the conclusion most people would leap to? And some guys just had roving eyes, a screw loose that way that nothing seemed to fix.

Still, Whit couldn't fathom how a guy would ever cheat on a woman with so much heart and passion. It didn't make sense.

All he really knew was that she'd obviously been badly hurt. And that he didn't want to add to that hurt.

"Dad?" Lilly poured a heaping bowl of cereal, no milk, and sat on her legs the way she always did. "What are we going to do today?"

"I figured we'd do some tree decorating. At least a little later."

"With what? We didn't bring any ornaments."

"I looked up some old traditions on the Net. We could string popcorn. And cranberries. Decorate with stuff like that. I also thought...how about if we make cookies? Starting with oatmeal raisin, your mom's favorite."

Pepper dropped her spoon and stared at him. Lilly raised the same stricken eyes her sister had.

"I didn't mean we had to do your mom's favorite," Whit said hastily. "I just figured you'd like making cookies. Lilly, you love—"

"Double chocolate chip."

Which he knew. "And Pepper—"

"My favorite's oatmeal raisin. Like Mom's."

Another silence fell with a clunk. No one seemed able to fill it.

Whit tried. "What about those cookies that are just plain? You know where you put the frosting on and sprinkles, like that."

"Those are sugar cookies, Dad." Lilly used her patient voice. The kind both eleven-year-old girls had opted to use with him for some time now. "And yeah, we could make those."

Thank God for Lilly. He wasn't sure if he was going to survive the girls' coming adolescence, but Lilly tended to say an exuberant yes to most ideas.

Pepper played with her cereal. "Are we really not going to do presents this year?"

Whit hated to answer. She hadn't taken off her first-of-the-morning scowl yet. "I thought we all agreed that this year—just this year—we'd do presents in a different way. Just buy some things that we could do together. Like games. Or an ice cream maker. I'd pop for new bikes—"

"What about cell phones?" Pepper piped in.

"No new cell phones. You have a cell phone."

"But we don't *both* have cell phones. And the one we have is boring. It doesn't *do* anything."

"Except call home in an emergency," Whit agreed.

"Dad! That's like what you have when you're six years old. We're way past that now."

"I know you both feel that way." Sometimes Whit had the worrisome feeling of being the mouse cornered by two cats. "But a lot of the new technology that costs a ton...we can't do all of it. So some of the fancy stuff, you have to be old enough to work, to earn some money yourselves, rather than count on me to pay for it."

Pepper opened her mouth to argue—this argument had been building for months now—but Lilly intervened, her voice careful and quiet.

"Dad, I think your idea about an ice cream maker

is way awesome. But still. I don't want to wake up Christmas morning with no presents, no surprises at all. Pepper and I like different things these days. We *need* different things these days."

"If you really need something, just tell me. That doesn't have to be about Christmas. I'm pretty sure we can always find a way to do something you really need."

Lilly's lip started to tremble, which meant her emotions were threatening to get away from her, but she obviously had something she wanted to say. "Even before Mom died, we were talking about redoing our room. Or using the study, so we could both have our own rooms. Pepper still wants purple, but I don't. I want blue. I could paint it myself."

Whit didn't have tics. But sometimes he felt like he could easily develop a few when his daughters tossed him in quicksand and he had no rule book about how to get out. "I don't have a problem with your having separate rooms. I didn't know about that. But that has nothing to do with Christmas."

"But it would have. If Mom were here. Because it'd be about coordinating colors of bedspreads and rugs and stuff on the wall. Figuring it out, then doing it together. And shoes. And my school jacket...it's just gorpy now."

"Gorpy," Whit echoed carefully.

"I'm not mad at you or anything," Lilly said. "But you just don't understand."

"I'm trying, honey—"

Too late. Her face had scrunched up, tight and red, the way it did when she was trying hard—too hard—not to cry. She bolted from the chair and ran upstairs before he could try to talk her down.

Pepper ducked her head, mainlined the cereal.

All he could think was that he was way, way over his head. He'd chosen the holiday away so they wouldn't be so constantly reminded of their mom. But nothing ever seemed simple with the twins. It wasn't just their mom they'd lost. But a woman in their lives. A grownup female's influence.

He could buy fifty ice cream makers and he still couldn't come through the way they needed sometimes. Bedspreads? How was he supposed to make getting a bedspread—a color coordinated bedspread—something he could do with his daughters?

He could probably do it.

Hell, he could probably volunteer for a root canal, if it was something good for his girls.

But hell's bells. Sometimes talking with them was like translating a language from New Guinea.

He needed help.

Chapter Five

Years ago, Rosemary had discovered that one of the best places to hide out was a darkroom—figuratively and literally. She wasn't thinking about Whit when she turned out the lights. Or her ex. Or Christmas. Or anything else but her work.

The photograph slowly clarifying in the tray was never going to make National Geographic quality, but that couldn't be helped. She remembered taking it; she'd been deep in the woods, on her stomach, in a pouring rain last summer when she spotted the orchid.

From the far room, she heard the landline ring. She ignored it. She couldn't answer either her cell phone or the lodge's landline when she was in the darkroom. Months before, she'd rigged up an answering device in the darkroom so she could catch messages, but there was no way she could reply without risking the work.

Muddy-browns gradually cleared. Background

greens gradually sharpened. Raindrops on the camera lens hurt the picture—but still, there she was. A tiny pale yellowish flower, with an even tinier white lip.

The species was the small whorled pogonia—a treasure because she was probably the rarest orchid in the eastern U.S. Finding her had been sheer, wonderful luck. The word *orchid* came from the Greek *orchis,* which meant testicle, not that Rosemary mentioned that particularly often in public. The point, though, was that particular shape was a key to identifying species that had orchid characteristics. Like this bitsy whorled pogonia...

The speaker in the corner of the wall registered the answering machine going on, then a hang up.

She returned to developing her baby. Some people called the plant "little five-fingers." If she hadn't found it flowering in late June, likely she'd never have spotted it ever. She wasn't that pretty, but she was *so* unique, and these days, so close to complete extinction.

The telephone rang again. She ignored it again.

Analyzing the testicle shape as the photograph developed to its clearest potential, was not, perhaps, the best way to keep her mind on serious subjects. Not that she was particularly interested in testicles. Or that she ever spent time thinking about testicles, for that matter.

But they were, after all, boy parts. And analyzing boy parts inevitably made her think of the human kind—not that she'd ever wasted daydreaming hours wondering about men's apparatus. Or that she'd ever spent time thinking about an individual man's apparatus, either.

But Whit, she couldn't help but remember, had expressed an inordinate amount of enthusiasm, pressed against her. That moment kept ripping through her consciousness. Feeling his arousal. The sudden thrill, the sudden sense of danger sending blood shooting up and down her pulse.

And there was his voice on the answering system. "I hung up a moment ago, Rosemary. It's me, Whit. I figured you're busy if you can't answer, and that's all right. Just need to leave a message. Here's the thing."

He cleared his throat.

Then cleared his throat again.

She lifted the soaking photo from the tray, hung it up with clothespins, tried not to breathe. When he said nothing else, she wasn't certain if he'd hung up or if she couldn't hear him—or if something else was wrong.

But he finally spoke again. "Okay, here's the truth. I'm in trouble. I wasn't going to call you this quickly after yesterday. I was afraid I may have overstepped some boundaries. I didn't want to make you uncomfortable. But this is different. I'm not kidding about being in trouble. Terrible trouble."

Again, he cleared his throat.

"It's the girls. It's about trying to have a Christmas and my goofing it all up. And somehow it's become about comforters or bedspreads or color coordinating or something like that. The twins…I'm used to them double-teaming me. But when they both completely confuse me, I just plain don't know how to dig my way out."

She couldn't answer the phone, still couldn't leave the darkroom, but the first smile came on strong, then a chuckle.

"I guess this is about shopping. Look. I won't do anything, won't say anything, won't touch even your hand, nothing. This is nothing about...that. But I'd pay you. A mortgage on your real house? A ruby or emerald or something? If you'd please go to Greenville with us tomorrow. I guess we could go to Traveler's Rest, but the girls seem to think we need to shop where there are more choices. Please. Please, Rosemary. I'm groveling. I'm desperate. I'm scared out of my skull. I can do teenage bras if and when I have to. But I can't color coordinate. I don't even get what that means. Please don't make me do this alone."

She wasn't sure whether he severed the call or her answering machine quit recording. Either way, he was off the line—and she let out a burst of a laugh.

Maybe if she could quit thinking of him as a lover, she could just enjoy what he had to offer. A friend. A caring dad with two daughters alone on a special holiday. Someone to have fun with. Someone to help him with the girls.

It wasn't as if she didn't have the free time...or didn't enjoy them all.

She just had to be careful about Whit. And she could do that.

Somehow she'd find a way to do that.

When Whit's SUV showed up the next morning, Rosemary dashed out. She opened the door, took one look at the expression on the two girls' faces and quickly glanced at Whit.

"Save me," he mouthed.

She popped into the front seat, and opened a travel

tote that was filled to bursting. "I brought catalogs," she told Lilly and Pepper. "So each of you could look through them, give me some idea about what you like and don't like."

As she latched her seat belt, she added to Whit, "Could you give me a general price range?"

He looked at her with the same trapped expression. "Whatever they want?"

She rolled her eyes, turned to the girls. "Where did your mom usually shop for clothes? Things around the house? Shoes?"

Neither had a problem answering the question, but Pepper came through with the most detail. "Mom liked to go on a shopping trip a couple times of year. She'd go to Atlanta or Dallas or like that. She liked Neiman Marcus. And Saks. Places like that."

She shot a startled look at Whit. She'd never envisioned his wife as being fancy and status-driven that way. "And those kinds of prices are okay with you?" she asked carefully.

"Is there something wrong?"

"No, not at all." Except that he was an earthy guy who worked with his hands and loved diving into projects headfirst. And the girls were describing a mom who was a dry-clean-only type of formal lady. She turned back to the girls. "We don't think we have any of those stores in Greenville, but there are still a ton of places to shop. In the meantime, I painted several rooms in the lodge when I moved there last June. Being me, I couldn't make up my mind, so I collected somewhere around five million paint swatches. So…"

Paint swatches came from the bottomless travel tote and were distributed to the backseat.

"You don't have to pick just one color. Pick, like, four or five. If you like blues, they don't have to be all blue. But I want you to choose colors that…well, that make you happy. Colors that you'd like to wake up to every morning. And then…"

She turned halfway, to include Whit in the conversation. "Then, I had another idea. If no one likes it, no problem. But possibly you might want to put up composite board or peg board or cork or something like that for one wall. That way, they'd have a place where they could hang their favorite rock stars or pictures or phone numbers or whatever they wanted. But they could also take down stuff and put up new without damaging the walls."

"Yeah! That's an awesome idea," Pepper said.

"I like it, too," Lilly agreed. The girls looked at each other as if astonished they'd agreed on anything—at least that day.

When Lilly handed back her choice of paint sample cards, they were all in blues and greens. Rosemary pushed her into a little more brainstorming. "Okay, is there something that you'd like to do with these colors? Such as…well, blues and greens make me think of water. The sea. Or I can imagine patterns of blues and greens—in paisley? Dots? Stripes? Paint swirls?"

When it was Pepper's turn, her choices were all violent oranges and reds. "Hmm, so you're not thinking restful. You like pops of color, right? So, we might find a comforter with red on one side, orange on the other. Or a bedspread with those colors in a pattern. Or…we could do white walls, with massive circles of orange and red…. Or do one wall orange, one red, then have white rugs, a white spread…?"

"Yeah, yeah!" If Pepper wasn't wearing a seat belt, she'd have been bouncing off the roof with excitement.

Rosemary felt Whit shoot her a sudden odd look—she wasn't sure why. So far, the trip seemed to be going far more smoothly than she'd thought at first glance. The girls had started out looking so huffy with each other, but they'd warmed up almost right away. She'd felt…well, not like a playmate with the eleven-year-olds. But not like a mother. More like an aunt—an aunt who didn't have to discipline or set rules or responsibilities. She could just…be with them. Be an adult female in their lives. Not intrude in any way that could hurt anyone.

She just had to be careful not to hurt Whit the same way.

She had no way to say anything private to him for quite a while. All roads were crowded with holiday traffic, and once they were inside the Greenville city limits, the congestion quadrupled.

Downtown Greenville, typically, was decorated within an inch of its life. Charity Santas rang bells at every corner. Lights sparkled in every doorway, on every tree; wreaths with red bows blessed every window. People hustled and bustled, frantic to get their last-minute shopping done. Whit likely found the last parking space in the county, and he'd barely locked the car before the girls cavorted ahead.

Rosemary stuck her hands in her pockets and

snugged next to him—not hip-bumping close—but near enough so he could hear her.

"Okay, before I worry it to death—how much of an apology do I owe you?" she asked.

"Apology? For what?" He did a good job of looking confused.

"I can go overboard. I know it. The thing is, I spent so much time with my two brothers that when I finally get around female company…well, I just really love some plain old girl time."

"You mean, like when the three of you were all talking at once and asking and answering questions at the same time?"

She grinned. "Yeah. Exactly that. And what a great definition for girl talk. But…honestly, I didn't mean to get carried away. I know you didn't want a commercial type of Christmas…"

"Are you kidding? Rosemary, I don't care what kind of Christmas we have, as long as the girls do something that doesn't make them sad. Besides, this whole business of redoing their bedrooms…I couldn't be happier you're doing this. For the past year, they stopped wearing the same clothes, stopped brushing their hair exactly the same way. I think it's a good thing, that they want their own sense of identity. I just didn't have a clue how to do the room thing. It just started coming up last year, around when their mom died."

"Still…"

"Still?"

"Well, I bumbled right into trouble—completely forgot to ask you ahead what you might want to budget for this, or how far you wanted me to go. When the girls mentioned Saks, I almost had a stroke."

"Because?"

She lifted her shoulders. "My parents made good money, even what most people would call darned good money. We never wanted for anything. But my mom used to say that if you wanted sheets more expensive than Penney's, you needed your head examined. We were a really busy family. Too busy to be dedicated consumers, I guess. But if your girls are used to shopping by brand, or by what's an 'awesome' brand…I probably won't know names like that."

He stopped dead, which she didn't realize until she glanced up and found him several steps behind her. He was staring at her so intently that she felt a flush— not outside, but inside—warm from her toes on up. "What?" she asked.

"Their mother was all about brands. Status. Appearance. Those things were important to her. I never put down Zoe in front of them, and never intend to. They loved her. She was devoted to them." He hesitated, and just as he started to say something else, the girls abruptly turned around and galloped back to them.

They spotted the first store they wanted to shop in.

The shopping adventure only took three hours… really, they all wanted to continue a little longer, but Whit started looking glassy-eyed and a little bit shell-shocked. Weak pulse, gray, lack of ability to focus. Rosemary may not have chosen a medical profession, but she'd seen men walking in malls before. The symptoms of an impending panic attack were unmistakable.

"Can we go home now? Are we done?" he asked

after the last purchase, which happened to be a quilt that Pepper fell for hook, line and sinker.

"I love it, I love it, I love it!" Pepper crowed. "It's way better than a comforter or a bedspread. It's all the colors I totally love—!"

"Can we drive home now?" Whit repeated, his voice the weakest of the four exchanging conversation.

She patted his hand, which couldn't conceivably be construed as a sexual gesture. "You did very, very well."

"Why isn't shopping recognized as an Olympic sport? Like triathlons or steeplechasing? You know, the kind of sport where you go through intensive training before you have to compete. The kind where you have to have proven athletic abilities to even survive. You three could all bring home medals." He added, "Could I lay down on the pavement now? I can't make it another step."

"You're so funny, Dad." Lilly crowded him with a massive hug on one side, Pepper on the other.

"Maybe the military could hire you three. The Marines are always looking for a few good men, but I suspect they've never met shoppers of your caliber.

"You could probably overthrow a country or two and still have energy left over."

"You'd better sit in the back with us, Rosemary. Trust us. He won't let up." This was whispered loudly from Pepper.

"Isn't there a medal of honor for surviving something like this?" Whit asked the world—as he dug out the key, unlocked and started heaping the packages in the back. "A purple heart. Or a bronze cross. Or maybe just a subtle *D* for *Dad* in neon lights. Or—"

Once the girls dissolved in giggles—and let loose with a few disgusted *"Daaaad"*s—he upped his pace.

"There must be some kind of training you females go through to build up your strength and endurance. And weight training. The tons in those packages in back is probably going to cost us extra mileage—assuming the tires can carry this much ballast. I'll bet you all do run-in-place exercises. Push-ups. Treadmill…"

Before they hit the second stoplight, the girls fell asleep, still strapped in, but limp as puppies, covered with blankets and jackets and packages. Whit glanced in the rearview mirror, realized why the girls were suddenly so quiet and quit with the teasing.

A few minutes later, he said suddenly, "Rosemary… I should have thought. We weren't far from the hospital complex in Greenville. If you'd wanted to stop to see your parents—"

She gave a wry chuckle. "Thanks, but not to worry. My chances of seeing them were probably around a zillion to one."

"That bad?"

She heard the humor in his voice. "Probably worse," she said, in the same humorous tone. "This is their home hospital. But they divide their time between here and Johns Hopkins—where they're always on call. They're both cardiac surgeons, but my mom specializes in small children. My dad works more with transplants, accident victims. Either way, when they're doing surgery, they're pretty much out of contact for five hours at a time or more. And if they're catching a few minutes shut-eye, no one will wake them. Not for a silly reason like a family member calling."

That silenced him, but not for long. "That was true, even when you were a child? That you couldn't reach them?"

She turned her head. He was watching traffic, not looking at her, but there'd been concern in his voice. Sympathy. "I don't think it hurt any of us, that our parents had important work...more important than thinking about us all the time. Besides, there were advantages to not having parents around much."

"Like?"

"Like...the three of us grew up self-reliant. If no one was around for dinner, I'd make a peanut butter and marshmallow sandwich."

He winced.

"Yeah, that's what my brothers thought, too. Ice cream in cereal was another one of my specialties. Sometimes with chocolate topping. Sometimes not."

"Chocolate topping. In the morning?"

"Hey, I'm talking about when I was eight or nine."

He shot her an amused look. She put her head back, and relaxed. Really relaxed, she realized. Shopping with the girls had been total fun, and shopping with Whit playing his suffering-guy act had been hysterical. They were so easy to be with.

Once out of Greenville, traffic lightened up, cars thinned out. Even though it was still afternoon, the sun had already started a fast slide toward the horizon.

"It gets dark so fast this time of year," she murmured, and glanced in the backseat again. "They're still sleeping."

It seemed only minutes later that the highway lights disappeared, and Whit reached the mountain turn-

off. He slowed down, and that quickly, they were surrounded by the lush green forests and winding around
the road's slithering curves. "Rosemary?"

When she turned her head at his curious tone, he
said, "Before we get to your place, I just want to say...
those were my daughters you met today. This is the
happiest I've seen them in a year. They were rowdy
and laughing and arguing and teasing each other, and
just...being *alive* again. Thanks. I mean it."

A lump clogged her throat. "I didn't do anything—"

"Yeah, you did. They lightened up with you. They
let loose. They even stopped being so darned good all
the time and came through with some serious sass. It
was all your doing."

The lump in her throat thickened. She couldn't help
it, any more than she could help feeling a wave of tenderness toward him. He seemed to see himself as a father, a widower, an ordinary guy.

She saw the rough jaw, the mesmerizing eyes, the
hard-honed muscled shoulders. She saw a man who
loved his kids deeply, beyond deeply. She saw a man
who was steadfast, who valued family, who seemed to
have no ego or awareness about his good looks. She
got it—that he was a good guy. But that wasn't what
rang her chimes.

Lust was.

Near him, she didn't feel a little tingle. She felt fire.
She heard sirens.

She heard herself yearning for him like a teenager
with a mortifying crush. And it had to stop. It was completely inappropriate and she knew it.

When he pulled up to her place, the girls were still

sleeping hard. Rosemary unbuckled her seat belt, grabbed her bag. Determined to act—to be—as normal around him as possible, she offered, "I'm not sure what I've got, but I could probably scare up some dinner."

"That's okay. I need to get home, get this car unpacked, get the girls settled in. They're scheduled for a Skype call to their grandparents still tonight."

"Your parents, or maternal grandparents?"

"Mine." He pushed the car into Park, then half turned to her. "I mean it, about thanking you. I don't want to embarrass you. I just want you to know how much today meant—for my girls, for us."

"Okay. That does it." She dropped her bag and swiveled toward him on one knee. "I've had it with you." He looked startled, then started to grin. Trying to maneuver over the console with its cupholders and gloves and debris was beyond awkward, but she managed it, managed to balance on one knee and pop a kiss on his mouth. She wanted to ham it up. Hoped she came across as silly and funny—anything to diminish those red-hot feelings for him, to reduce his effect on her down to a normal, livable level.

And she did.

Sort of.

Her lips smacked his then immediately lifted. She only caught a millisecond of his taste, his scent, those butter-soft lips of his. She avoided his eyes, grabbed her purse again, and then reared back to grab the door handle. "Quit with the thank-yous, or you'll be sorry," she said in her crossest voice. "I love spending time with your daughters. Loved spending your money. Loved getting out to do some Christmasy things instead of working."

"I'm sorry I thanked you," he said humbly.

"You should be."

"Are you going to kiss me if I do it again?"

Well, hell. She wanted a lighter feeling between them. Instead there was a glitter in his eyes that hadn't been there before. He had an expression, something like a rooster who just found the key to the henhouse—and she was the hen.

"No," she said. "Next time I'll whack you upside the head. You can count on it."

"And you can count on there being a next time, Rosemary."

She heard him say good-night as she closed the door and headed for the house. She didn't look back—not until she was inside and her jacket and bag had been thrown on the chair. Then she glanced out, watched until the headlights turned around, until he started downhill, until the last wink of his tail lights disappeared.

Then she took a long, deep breath.

There was no way she would hurt that vulnerable family.

No way she would hurt Whit. Which meant—lust or no lust—she would find some way to cool her jets around him, whatever it took.

Chapter Six

"Got to get you into my life...." Whit couldn't remember where the song came from, who sang it, what the rest of the words were. And he didn't care. That title showed up in his head, and like a guest at a party, refused to leave.

He felt that song was his plan for Rosemary. About the woman who kicked up his juices from here to Poughkeepsie. About the woman who engaged him, fascinated him, in ways his wife never had. Rosemary was like him. She liked natural things, no labels, no pretenses, no tickets to the opera. He knew she'd like a wandering hike on a fall-bitten day, knew she'd stop to love the sunshine dancing on a creek. Life with her would be fewer dinners with antique china, more picnics in the shade of an oak. Less ballet tickets and more lying outside and counting stars.

"Daaad! Would you quit humming that stupid tune?"

"I didn't know I was doing it," Whit defended.

Lilly said kindly, "We *know* you don't know what you're doing. Look at this mess."

He quit humming and looked. The afternoon project was supposed to be stringing popcorn to decorate the tree. His job, he figured, was making the popcorn. So he'd made it. And made some more. And then more—enough to fill every bowl, every plate, every pitcher in the place, and then to just kind of lay down newspaper to heap the rest.

"You think we have enough?" Whit asked Lilly.

His daughters exchanged glances. When the twins shared that kind of look, it made him terrified of their teenage years. One child was a child. Two children, especially twins, were a pack.

"Dad," Lilly said tactfully, "we have enough popcorn to decorate our tree, Rosemary's tree and probably every tree in Charleston. The problem is that now we have to string it."

"Well, of course. That's the idea."

"Uh-huh. Well, if you didn't pack some needles and thread, we sure didn't," Pepper informed him. "We didn't know we were going to do this."

Whit hadn't either...but normally he had an IQ higher than ten. Obviously they couldn't string garlands of popcorn without needle and thread—unless there was some unknown other way. "Maybe we could try glue?"

"Dad," Lilly said, again using her Be-Patient-With-Dad voice, "we don't have glue, either. We're not home. We don't have the stuff we have around home."

"And glue wouldn't work anyway," Pepper said. "I know what would, though."

"Me, too," Lilly agreed.

"What?" Whit was all ears.

"What we need to make this work is…" Both girls finished the sentence in unison. *"Rosemary."*

"Well, darn," Whit said in a tone of complete meek astonishment. "You two just might be right."

"So could we call her, Dad? Could we?"

"She could come over, help us string the popcorn. Maybe watch a movie with us? Like why *not*, Dad?"

"Well…I don't know. Maybe if you two called her—"

"Yeah! We'll call her right now!"

He did his best to be talked into the plan. Then he did his best to heave himself in the overstuffed chair and look helpless, as he watched the girls grabbing the phone from each other, bouncing around as they talked to Rosemary. Pepper knocked over a glass with drops of milk still left in it. Lilly punched her when Pepper refused to give over the phone.

He wasn't sure what Rosemary was saying…but he was positive the girls could talk her into coming over if anyone in the universe could.

He noted the spilled milk, the knocked over glass, the array of blankets on the couch from where the girls had curled up watching TV the night before, the splash of shoes and scarves strewn in the general vicinity of the back door.

He couldn't help but think of Zoe's reaction. She would have hated everything about this place, would see it as a household out of control—a sin on a par with murder or grand theft, and a lack of manners.

Twenty minutes later, Rosemary came through the front door with her arms full of bags. She heeled off her boots, held her car key between her teeth so she could divest herself of parcels and get her jacket off. Instead of her usual cherry parka, she wore a soft, fuzzy jacket in the girls' favorite purple.

The girls rushed her with the exuberance of defense after the opening kick. Both tried on her jacket—with her permission—the whole time they nonstop chattered. From the parcels and bags, she produced a plastic bag of thread, a container of sewing needles, two bottles of whole cloves, a bag of fresh oranges, fresh lemons, a linen bag of herbs he could smell from the door and a gallon—no, two gallons—of cider.

Whit suddenly suspected that he'd been demoted from manager of the day's events to unpaid flunky.

When she had everything—but the kitchen sink—*on* the kitchen sink, she finally had both hands free. She smooched Lilly on the cheek, then Pepper on the forehead, then loped over, went up on tiptoe, and gave him a fast smooch on the chin.

A kiss like she gave the kids.

Like he was another kid.

He'd never guessed before that she had a cruel side.

"Whit, can you bring in the big pot from my car? Oh, and there's a giant spoon ladle thing on the seat. And there might be another grocery sack…."

The day turned into a marathon honey-do list. Outside, a thready drizzle turned into a window-drumming downpour. The girls turned on a chick flick for background—something about knights and that kind of junk. He was given sets of instructions. Slice lemons and oranges. Put the pot on the stove, pour in the cider, add the linen bag of herbs, start stirring, don't let it boil, keep stirring, add the lemons and oranges, keep stirring.

The girls got the stringing popcorn job. Actually, he offered, but the three females pounced on him when they caught him—it was only one time!—nibbling on the popcorn instead of stringing it. They gave him another god-awful chore after that. He was supposed to stick cloves in oranges. Like cover up the orange completely with cloves. That was interesting for almost three or four minutes, but then his fingertips started hurting from all the clove stabbing, and he couldn't get them in straight anyway.

He complained that his hands were too big for this particular job.

No one paid him any attention.

He continued killing his fingers on the cloves. Continued stirring the wassail. And in the meantime, watched her listen to his girls, really listen, even for answers to the simplest questions she asked them.

She started out by asking what their mom used to like for Christmas like what kind of presents. Did they ever make things by hand, or did their mom give them ideas, or how did they all work it?

"Well, Mom always made it easy for us. She'd ask for a Dior lipstick or something like that, that Pepper and I could afford by splitting."

"Yeah," Pepper agreed. "But with Dad, she'd give him a whole list. Like a new Coach purse or a Movado watch or two days at a fancy spa—Mom loved that kind of thing."

"And jewelry. She loved jewelry. But she always said men couldn't buy jewelry because they didn't understand what a woman wanted, so she'd pick that out for herself. Just put it on Dad's card."

Pepper added, "So she made it easy on everybody. She could get exactly what she wanted, but nobody had to do anything hard. Dad hates shopping, so he really liked it that way."

Rosemary's back was turned away from his view, so Whit couldn't see her face or read her expression, but her voice took on a different tone. "Okay…so how do you know what to pick out for your dad?"

"Oh, Dad's *really* easy. He always wants tools and stuff like that. And besides, he likes surprises. Like I got him a polka-dotted flashlight one year. Cracked him up. But it was a good light, you know? He used it all the time."

Lilly piped in, "And I got him a big bowl one time. It was for his popcorn. He always said that Mom's china was too darned fancy for a football popcorn afternoon, and there wasn't a big bowl in the whole house. He used that all the time, too."

"And we both made him ties one year in school. I can't remember what they were made of, but we dunked them in this swirl of dye. So everybody's was different. I mean, all the ties were made the same way. But each one had different colors, different swirls."

Lilly jumped in again. "The thing is, Dad doesn't like ties. He never wore ties for anything unless Mom made him. But he liked the ones *we* made. If he picked us up from school or was going to teachers' meetings or something, he *always* wore one of our ties."

"He said we saved him from all the god-awful ties out there in the stores."

"And then Mom'd yell at him for saying god-awful. But we knew what he meant. Ties are pretty boring."

"Father's Day was different, though," Pepper interrupted. "Dad always said he didn't want a present. So we'd try to think of something to do with him. Like we cooked him breakfast even when we were *really* little. Like sometimes adding a maraschino cherry to scrambled eggs. With maybe some peanut butter. And he *ate* it."

"And one Father's Day we said we'd mow the lawn for him. But we couldn't really use the riding mower by ourselves. So Dad mowed while we just hung on. That was fun."

"And sometimes we'd sneak out to get McDonald's or Burger King for Father's Day. Because Mom didn't like that kind of food. And he loves it."

Okay, they had to be boring her ears off. Whit quit listening…but he couldn't seem to stop watching.

The girls glommed on to Rosemary as if she was the rose and they were the bees. They never stopped talking. She'd got them talking about Christmas—when he'd been afraid to do that—but they didn't get upset, mentioning their mom. Not with Rosemary. She just made it…natural somehow.

The three females had claimed the couch, all sewing strings of popcorn. Three pairs of loose socks were perched on the coffee table, not much different in size. All three had blond hair, although the girls had thicker, longer styles, where Rosemary's was short. Still, scooched down, heads against the couch back, the three looked as if they belonged together. Belonged like a family. Free to be yourself—that kind of comfortable. That kind of belonging.

The house filled up with smells. Pine, cloves, oranges. Outside the rain stopped, leaving a glistening cold afternoon. He brought out sandwiches and mugs of wassail. The group weaved their garlands of popcorn on the tree, then strung his cloved-oranges from wherever they could find a hook—lamp arms, window latches, wooden chandeliers.

More smells showed up after that—almond and cinnamon. The girls destroyed the kitchen, leaving flour and crusty bowls everywhere, and eventually sheets of snickerdoodles emerged from the oven, finally cooled enough to devour. After that came a couple batches of sugar almond cookies.

The females claimed they were too tired to clean up—naturally, when the kitchen was in such bad shape the health department would likely have condemned it. He let them get away with it. It wasn't that hard to hurl stuff in the dishwasher, swipe down counters, wrap up cookies.

When he finished, he ambled to the doorway. They'd all moved to the floor by the Christmas tree. Rosemary was lying on her side, the curve of her hip a fabulous view for a man who was already fiercely, helplessly smitten. The conversation had turned mighty serious, seemed to be about the icky boys in their class, the unfair teachers.

He strolled forward, making enough noise so they

knew they were being interrupted, and gave each a slight whip with the dish towel. "We've been inside all day. Time for a walk."

The young ones took out their usual bag of complaints. It was too wet. Too cold. They were too tired. They were happy right where they were.

"Did I just do the dishes for you all? Did I sample your cookies so you could be sure they weren't poisoned? Did I make the wassail? Did I carry the trees in?"

They conceded to a *short* walk. *Very* short. The agreement only came after hard-won union negotiations—their union consisting of the two of them, and no one in the universe could out-negotiate his twins. They wanted to watch some chick flick the following Tuesday that was just coming out. They wanted a sleepover after the first of the year.

They were still tacking on demands as he coaxed them toward their jackets and gloves and shoes—still fine-tuning the details, when he opened the door and delicately pushed them all out. It was like herding cats. They could do spin moves. Evasive tactics. He resorted to carrying Pepper upside down, which was guaranteed to make them both shriek nonstop.

When he finally had all three outside, he turned a beleaguered sigh on Rosemary. "They're monsters. You'd think they'd been raised by wolves."

She was no help. Her cheeks were already pink from laughing so hard. He obviously wasn't going to get any sympathy from her, but damn…she was gorgeous when she laughed. Her eyes picked up sparkle, her skin seemed to glow.

"You have so much fun with them!"

He raised his eyebrows. "Of course I have fun with them. What's the point of having kids if you can't torment them now and then?"

"That's not every parent's attitude."

"I know. But I never understood it. Why people have kids if they don't want to spend time with them."

Talk came easily, nothing demanding or heavy. Outside was a shine-soaked afternoon. The chill had a bite, but raindrops hung on branches like teardrops. Pine needles carpeted the old woods, all washed clean from the midday rain. The house smells had been fabulous, enticing.... The fresh oxygen outside was also enticing, just in a different way. Whit needed that blast of sharp air to clear his head.

Although he already knew what he wanted to do.

The girls pranced on ahead. The gravel path down the mountain was easy to follow, trails just as easily marked. The woods up here were virgin, old, big-trunk trees shadowing out any smaller growth—which made it ideally easy to suddenly, carefully grab Rosemary's hand. A little twist, beyond a tree or two, then a dance behind pines, and he had her alone. Maybe only for seconds, and not far from the girls. But he still had her alone.

He took her mouth. Right then. Fast. Before she had a clue what was coming.

He did. He'd known all day, maybe knew from the minute he'd met her, that something was there between them. Maybe it had to be uncovered, searched for, worked for—but he had an absolutely clear vision about what he wanted to do with and for and to Rosemary MacKinnon.

He was going for treasure.

At first, she went tense in his arms.

At first.

The wind picked up a sudden bit. So many scents surrounded them—the tang of pine, the rich scent of wet earth and stinging fresh air. And her. Covered in that fluffy purple jacket of hers, all zipped up...but her lips suddenly parted for his. Her headed tilted back, and she lifted up, lifted into him, her arms swooping around his neck.

Aw, man.

She didn't kiss like a good girl. She kissed like maybe this was her last chance, the last chocolate in the box, and she was going to savor the best damned kiss with everything she had. She made a sound. A soft sweet sound of yearning, a sound so vulnerable and naked that he felt a silver streak of need.

She wasn't any woman. This wasn't any kiss. It was a connection. The kind that made him want to own her—and to be owned right back. To have lusty, wild, sweaty sex...and then take all night, making tortuously tender love. He desperately wanted to hold her through the night. He fiercely needed to protect her through a life.

His hands slid around her, down her back, down to her butt...felt a fierce resentment at all the darned clothes between them. He needed to feel her. All of her. He was too old to invite this kind of frustration, even if it was a hurt-so-good kind of pain. He just didn't want to let her go.

A sudden rustling sound broke through his closed-eyes concentrated exploring of her mouth.

The sound didn't immediately stop him. It wasn't some alien wild animal rustling...it was eleven-year-old girls type of rustling. His twins were close—but they hadn't discovered them yet. He still had a few more seconds. He didn't want to give up even a millisecond of these kisses, these touches. With her.

But Rosemary heard Pepper's voice and suddenly sprang back, her eyes glazed and startled. For an instant he saw an unguarded look on her face, in her eyes. She wanted him. Maybe it took a stolen, breathless kiss to unlock that truth from the closet, but he wasn't the only one with feelings. He wasn't the only one who'd never expected an avalanche of emotion and need out of the complete blue.

"Whit," she started to say. From unguarded vulnerability, she turned on the repression button, snapped that attitude into her voice.

But the girls suddenly showed up in sight, and galloped toward them, chattering and yelling the whole way. "Da-ad! You said a *short* walk! And now we did it and we're starving. And exhausted. And Lilly lost a mitten."

"I did not."

"It was *my* mitten and you took it and now it's disappeared!"

"Because you dropped it in the woods, you numb-skull!"

He interjected carefully, "If you don't scare off Rosemary with your arguing, I was thinking about asking her to come back home with us, have dinner."

"We're not arguing anymore." Pepper elbowed her sister in the ribs. Lilly elbowed her right back and added a hair pull. Both gleamed beatific smiles at Rosemary.

She opened her mouth as if to say no to the dinner, then shot a quick careful glance at him. "Okay," she said, but she was still looking at him.

She wasn't coming back because of food. She was coming back, he strongly suspected, because she planned on straightening him out about a few things.

Rosemary wasn't one to duck or deny a problem.

But then, neither was he.

Once home, the girls—led by Rosemary, of course—threw him out of the kitchen and insisted they were making dinner…and "he'd better not complain."

A brilliant way to avoid any one-on-one time with him, Whit figured. But it wasn't as if he minded getting a chance to put his feet up in the recliner, catch some news, and half listen to the clatter of pots and splash of water and nonstop giggling from the kitchen. He'd known, when he pushed this holiday week in the mountains on the girls, that it wouldn't be easy. They "played" with him. They had fun with him. But it wasn't the same as having friends or female company around.

He'd fiercely not wanted them to have a grieving, sad Christmas, not have Zoe on their minds all the time, not get swallowed up by that kind of sadness. No matter what issues came up here, he'd been pretty sure anything would be better than staying at home. And it was.

But having Rosemary around brightened up the twins more than a cache of gold. She wasn't like their mom. She was just…herself. But if he could have bought a present that really mattered for his daughters this holiday, it'd be her. Rosemary.

"Dinner, Dad!" Pepper announced, carrying a platter in from the kitchen. Apparently they weren't eating at the table. The menu started with raw carrots, cut in curls. Peanut butter and banana sandwiches. Chips. A plate of cheese, each piece cut in squares or triangles or circles. And, of course, three kinds of cookies.

The biggest plate was the cookies.

The kids ate like vultures. So did Rosemary. The three of them took credit for putting together a totally junk food meal, but Rosemary couldn't look at him with a straight face when she claimed that. After dinner, the paper plates disappeared, the kitchen got wiped down, and when Rosemary said she really needed to get back home, the girls swooped on her for hugs... after which Pepper claimed she was going to wash her hair and Lilly was disappearing upstairs to check her email and Facebook.

Rosemary said she was getting her jacket, but she was gone for a bit. Whit figured she'd run into the bathroom. Whatever, he crouched down, started building a Boy Scout fire, the laying of the kindling just so, striking the flame, blowing just a little to help it catch. The fruitwood he'd brought in did a perfect burn, adding to the great scents in the house already.

"What a perfect end to a great day...a warm fire. Especially next to the tree that's *almost* starting to look like a real Christmas tree," Rosemary suddenly said, striding in from the back hall with her purple jacket on and already zipped to the throat.

He didn't need a crystal ball to get the message—

she was making a run for the nearest exit. No way she was staying. No way she was risking any more kisses with him today.

Zoe had always told him that he wasn't the brightest. But when it came to basic communication, Whit always figured he got an A plus. The worry in Rosemary's eyes told a complete story that started with *n* and ended with *o*.

He lurched to his feet, dusted his hands on the seat of his jeans. "I'll walk you out to your car."

"No need!"

"That's okay. I need a second of fresh air." He kept his hands in his pockets, just so Rosemary could see he was behaving himself. He trailed her out the door, latched it, and then jailed his hands in pockets again. The sky was black and silent as a promise. She dug in her bag for her car key.

"Rosemary, I can't thank you enough for the day. You don't need me to tell you how much fun the girls had with you. You're beyond great with kids."

"Thanks." She shot him a grin. "It's not hard to be great with great kids. Especially when I don't have to be the disciplinarian."

"You'd probably be great with that, too." He scuffed a heel in the gravel drive. "Any plans for kids of your own down the pike?"

The grin on her face froze. "Not likely." Her tone stayed light and easy, but something was there, in that glued-on grin, in her eyes. "It seems I have skinny tubes. Found out in a physical last year. It's not impossible for me to get pregnant, but the chances are around one in a zillion, or so they tell me."

Now it was his turn to freeze up. He'd never guessed he was putting a foot in it. Hell. He'd never have asked her a hurtful question if he'd known. "I'm sorry."

"Me, too. No point in lying about it. I took it hard. On the other hand, being an aunt gives me lots of kid time. My one brother's due his first baby in a couple months…and my other brother has boys, two, just about Pepper and Lilly's age. My theory is that an aunt should be able to spoil kids, give them noisy presents like drums and percussion instruments, take them places their parents never would. It's all payback for my brothers. And the older I get, the more involved I can get. I'd like to take them on the Appalachian Trail. Maybe Alaska. Maybe a hike in Europe. When they get older anyway…."

She was easy to talk to. He liked hearing it all. But he couldn't get it out of his head, that she couldn't have kids. That she'd found out not long ago. He'd known there was a heavy secret related to the bozo, because he couldn't imagine Rosemary dumping a guy right before the wedding on a whim. So…he never wanted to pry, never intended to, but somehow the question blurted out before he could stop it. "Rosemary…was that it? Why you broke off the relationship with the man you were engaged to? Because he wanted kids and you couldn't have them?"

She'd opened the driver's door, tossed her bag inside, was a pinch away from climbing in and turning the key. But now she stopped. Said nothing for a breadth of a second.

"Hell," he mumbled. "I'm sorry, Rosemary. None of that's any of my business. I just…"

"It's all right. Really." She climbed in and latched the seat belt before looking at him again. Her face was in shadow. "You know what's funny? That's exactly what I'd been afraid of, when I told George—that he'd be really upset if we couldn't naturally have kids. But his response was the total opposite. He didn't care. At all. In fact, I realized pretty quickly that he was actually happy about it. Now it seems obvious to me that was a clue."

"A clue?"

She hesitated, and then shook her head. "Whit, I don't mind talking about this sometime, but not tonight. We've had such a good day. So did your girls. And it's just two days until Christmas Eve now…so if you're all not tied up tomorrow, I have an idea for you three."

"We're not remotely tied up."

"I have some work I really want to do, but could I stop over after lunch? I was thinking…the girls might like to make a manger. You know. Like…create a shelter out of boughs, use things we find in the woods to make a crèche, a Nativity scene. Not buy anything. Just work with things we find in nature?"

"Wonderful idea. I love it."

But as she drove away, he thought what he loved… was her. He kept telling himself that he'd only known her for days, but every minute with her, every second, seemed richer than the last. His life seemed bigger than before he met her. Bigger with possibilities. With hope. With excitement over what could be.

When her taillights disappeared, he turned back to the house.

The mystery of her broken engagement was more

troubling than ever. That she was unlikely to have a
baby was impossibly sad for a child lover like her...
but that information only made Whit more concerned
at what the son of a sea dog had done that so devastated her.

He wasn't sure he had a chance...unless she was
past that hurt.

Chapter Seven

Rosemary had glued her behind to the desk chair, determined to get some work done before going over to Whit's—and for darned sure, before allowing herself to think about the man. Outside, the sun poured down, not a puff of cloud in the whole darned sky—a perfect day to be outside, tromping around, breathing in the sweet mountain air.

Instead she was working on ovaries.

Photographs were spread out over a door—literally a door. No table was large enough to display the photographs, not when she needed to see the whole kit and caboodle to determine the proper order. Whether each orchid was beautiful or plain, huge or tiny, each one needed to be identified as either male or female. Often enough, finding the ovary required a serious magnifying glass.

She'd discovered something unexpected in her research. The girl orchids who did the best job of hiding or protecting their ovaries seemed to be the strongest survivors.

Maybe that was why she had skinny tubes? Because she didn't have what it took to be a good survivor? At least after George had kicked her in the emotional teeth, and made her feel like less than a woman.

Would you quit? Stop thinking about men and life and get your mind back on sex.

She was trying. Studying a photograph of the Zygopetalum, she tucked a leg under her and measured the darling's ovaries…and the big lip designed to attract a lusty insect. Measuring the size of the ovaries in proportion to the lip size was taking many hours of painstaking work. The results were fascinating—at least to her. It just took so many exacting, grueling hours that she was starting to fear she'd get blisters on the brain.

When she heard her cell phone sing, she sprang up faster than a criminal let loose from jail.

"Hey, Rose. How's my favorite hermit doing?"

Tucker, God love him, only insulted her when he was too far away to be whacked upside the head. "Doing good. How's marriage? How're my nephews?"

"That's partly why I'm calling. To tell you that UPS seemed to deliver a truckload of Christmas presents here for my monsters. And also to tell you that you might need a bigger truck next year."

"Oh, wow, oh, wow. You mean Garnet's expecting? I'm so excited! Boy or girl, do you know? And when's it due? And how's Garnet feeling? And—"

"Wait a minute. I need to get in a word, too." She heard Ike's voice, which meant the brothers were conference calling her. They only did that when they wanted to gang up on her about something. She carried the phone into the kitchen, where she found the stupid coffeepot was empty and the maid hadn't shown up to refill it.

Oh. She didn't have a maid. Sometimes she forgot.

Ike said, "I've got a little one in the oven, too, you know. And a bride who's going to have Christmas with the MacKinnons for the first time. Rosemary, come on. You could help her like no one else."

"I can smell guilt in the air." Rosemary measured the coffee—more or less. Then added cold water and set the machine to brew. "Both of you might as well pour it on."

"Well, I'm in the same situation. Garnet's met the parents. But her parents are pretty terrifying, so Christmas overall is going to be an extra test of nerves for her. If you could just come for one afternoon. Christmas Day. We'd all be there."

"And we'd miss you. Not just the wives. Us. We're your only brothers, remember? And I know you've been nonstop badgered by the parents." Tucker always went straight to the point. "But we'd be there as buffers. And the idea of you spending a holiday alone just plain sucks—"

"I won't be alone."

There. Silence. "Say that again," Ike insisted.

She glanced at the clock. Whit wouldn't expect her until after lunch, and it was only ten-thirty. She had more than enough time to change into extra warm clothes, fix herself a sandwich, maybe see if she could remember where she'd buried her makeup from six months ago. Not that she was thinking about Whit. Or that she cared what she looked like when the four of them were doing nothing but tromping around the woods.

"Are you talking about the guy you mentioned the other day? The one renting the place down the mountain?" Tucker didn't like to waste time in between questions.

"Yes. The same one. The one who has twins, daughters. They lost their mom last year just before Christmas—"

"Yeah, I remember your telling me."

"Well, no one told me," Ike complained. "So…this guy is obviously single, then?"

"It's not like that," she said firmly. "It's just…we hit it off. All of us. Started doing holiday things together. I feel like…well, like I have the chance to make a good Christmas for them."

"Hey, that's all cool. So…what's he doing for a job? Making any kind of good living? Is he ugly as a rock? Good-looking?—"

"Ike!" God, having two brothers was sometimes a test of faith. Or patience. Or both. "He has two vulnerable kids."

"Yeah, well Garnet and I had two vulnerable kids, and you know how that worked for us." Tucker had a certain tone in his voice. The kind of tone a dog got when someone tried to take his bone. He wasn't going to give up on this easily.

She poured coffee. Added sugar. Then remembered that she didn't take sugar, and turned to face the window.

"Guys. I'll be part of the family again after the holiday. I love you both. I'm going to miss you more than you can imagine—and the kids. And even Mom and

Dad. But I just need this time to myself, okay? And finding a family that needed help is just what the doctor ordered—no pun intended about the doctor metaphor."

"You haven't slept with him, have you?"

"Let's tone that down," Ike chided his brother, only then proceeded to attack from the same side of the fence. "Has he kissed you? Got to first base? Second? How far as this gone?"

"I've only known him less than a week!"

"She isn't answering the question," Ike said to Tucker. "You want me to go up there?"

"We could both—"

"No. No, no, no. Would you quit it? I don't need babysitting or big brother advice. I'll see all of you after the holiday. That's a matter of days, not years. I need to be here. Would you try to believe me?"

Neither spoke for a moment, which told Rosemary she was finally winning the argument.

Tucker said finally, "Here's the thing, Rosemary. The longer you won't talk to the parents about George, the more they worry that something unforgettably traumatic happened to you. I only see one way that's going to change, and that's for you to spend some time with them, let them see that you're okay and doing fine. The holiday's the easiest time to do that, because the rest of us will all be there."

Rosemary pinched her nose. Man, she was sick of keeping the damned secret. If it was just for her sake, she'd have spilled the reason for the broken engagement eons ago. Unfortunately, it was for her parents' sake that she'd kept quiet. They didn't know she was protecting them. How could they?

"Guys," she said carefully. "I need you to trust me. I'd walk on water for you two. I already know you'd do the same for me. But I can't participate in a regular holiday this year. Please just let it go."

They both said "sure," but Rosemary knew perfectly well they didn't mean it. She had to find a better answer than silence, but so far she couldn't think of a way to explain what happened with George without embarrassing and troubling a whole lot of people.

Once she'd severed the call, she put it out of her mind. She wasn't the only one who had reasons to feel vulnerable this holiday. Pepper and Lilly mattered a whole lot more than her problems. Her trouble was just an "issue." The girls had lost their mom.

And Whit had lost his wife.

With another quick glance at a clock, she charged into action. She grabbed a cheese sandwich while she chased down hiking boots, exchanged a sweatshirt for a blue alpaca sweater, brushed her hair, slapped on gloss, filled a thermos with coffee and grabbed her keys. Naturally she had to run back in the house to turn off the coffeepot. Then back again to grab some serious gloves.

The drive to Whit's place took less than five minutes…but it was enough time to give herself a stern mental talking-to. She'd been making too much over those kisses in the woods yesterday.

Twice now, he'd taken her by surprise. Twice now—she admitted it—he'd taken her breath away. And twice now, she could have gone with those stupendous emotions and made love with him. It wouldn't be that hard to put aside morals and hurts and life issues—even Pepper and Lilly, because they didn't have to know. And yeah, there were other major things, like that he lived in Charleston—and she didn't. For sure her life was more flexible than his; down the pike she could relocate to all kinds of places. But none of those were the most serious reason she needed to get a grip and behave herself.

He was a wounded, grieving husband.

She saw two heads in the window when she turned the knob, saw both girls bob around, as if yelling to their dad that "she's here!"

Next thing she knew, the three of them tumbled out with a chorus of greetings. She met Whit's eyes over the kids—and yeah, she felt the *whoop* in her pulse. But sharing a smile with him was about more than that whoop factor. He loved it that his girls were so excited, so happy. He was on her team; she was on his. The look he gave her was a heartwarmer, not just a lustwarmer.

He steered them toward the Gator. His jacket was eons old, a serious outside work jacket, well loved, and as brawny as he was. "Has anyone even asked Rosemary her plan on how to make our manger?"

Since she'd thought up the idea on the spur of the moment, she wasn't exactly prepared with a complex plan. She said, "Well, first, we should pick a site close to your house, so you can see it from the windows. And we need to be careful that the project isn't too complex—we don't want to have a nightmare to take apart after the holiday."

She got two thumbs up, then had to grapple for more plan ideas. "Well…I was just thinking that we'd start gathering twigs and sticks. We'd start building them in a crisscross pattern, the way Boy Scouts are taught to make a fire? Only in our case, we want to make the shape of a cradle."

Yup. Everybody agreed they could do that. Only the three of them were still looking at her, and she was fresh out of ideas. "And after that," she said brightly, "your dad will figure out how to make the shelter around it."

She got her hair ruffled for that, which made the girls laugh. She pretended to slug Whit in retaliation, but that made them laugh even harder. There was something in Whit's eyes that had nothing to do with horseplay and teasing...something hot enough to take the chill out of the brisk, windy day.

But she didn't trust her judgment about Whit, not anymore, and besides that the girls were happy. That's what the whole outing was about, something fun for them, something about the holiday—and hopefully about doing something they'd never done before, so there was no chance the project would remind them of sad memories.

And it worked so well. The temperature tried to warm up, and the winter sun valiantly tried to shine. Leaves crackled and squirrels scattered, shocked by all the human noise and silliness. Rosemary participated, but she watched, too, loving how Whit razzed the girls, how they teased him in return.

The girls kept running back to the house, because they "needed things." And Whit had the toughest job, creating a "shed" with boughs draped over long sticks. Eventually Rosemary and the girls finished the crèche. Sort of. The cradle looked like a cradle, as Lilly put it, if you were standing upside down and were really near-sighted. They'd made the baby from rags and twine, a doll that fit exactly in the twig manger. A kitchen towel worked as a blanket.

But then Lilly fretted that they didn't have a Mary and Joseph or any wise men. She and Pepper charged back in the house, brought back billowing bed sheets, and then more twine and rubber bands, to make them into human characters. Whit said, "Did you guys really bring all the sheets off the bed? What on earth are we going to sleep on tonight?"

But Whit was overruled. The female team already had a new quest. How could you put together a Nativity scene without gifts? Because the wise men—or wise guys, as Pepper put it—had brought "stuff" like frankincense and myrrh.

A long debate ensued over what on earth "myrrh" was. No one was sure—but they were all dead positive they didn't have any, so they had to come up with other gift ideas.

Lilly remembered there were fresh cranberries in the house. Lots of cranberries. More cranberries than they wanted to string for the tree—ever. Pepper had glitter shoes that didn't fit her anymore, even though they were almost new. Both girls had hairpins that sparkled. And they both had glow sticks that lit up when you cracked them. The heap of "gifts" kept building, until they were all tired. Whit called a halt, and they all stood back to assess their masterpiece.

"Magnificent," Rosemary pronounced. "For sure, the most original manger ever created."

"I'm afraid our wise men look a lot more like Halloween ghosts than people. Except for the baby. We did pretty good with the baby."

"Dad, you did the best with the shed. That really looks like a shelter. And now that the sun's going down, our glow lights look really awesome." Lilly said nothing more for a minute, but then from nowhere she came up with, "Man. Mom would really have hated this."

"What?" Rosemary's head whipped around. "Honey, why do you think so?"

Pepper did her classic shrug. "Mom liked things to look just so. And 'just so' pretty much meant like from Nordstrom's or Saks, you know? Tasteful. That was one of Mom's favorite words. *Tasteful. Expensive. Perfect.*"

Rosemary's heart sank. She'd hoped they were doing something they'd never done before…but the last thing she'd wanted was to do something "wrong" on their mom's terms. "But this was a different project than a traditional Christmas thing, don't you think? We weren't trying to do anything perfect. We didn't want to buy anything. We were trying to create something… well, personal…something we did with our own hands, our own effort."

Lilly patted her hand. "Rosemary, chill. It's awesome. We had a great time doing it. We're just saying that Mom wouldn't have liked it, that's all."

Whit came from behind, hooked an arm loosely around her shoulder. "Come on, team. Sun's going down, and the temperature's dropping like a stone. Not even counting that, I'll bet we're all starved."

She glanced up, but he didn't look back at her. His expression was distant, distracted. Perhaps he hadn't heard the girls' comments about their mom. She felt the warmth and weight of his arm around her shoulders, thinking that it felt so darned right to be snugged close to him. To be in touch with him. To feel his warmth, his protectiveness. And yeah, to feel enough sizzle to start a bonfire.

How crazy was that? And when the girls started talking, she felt the glow disappear from the afternoon completely.

They weren't far from the house, but the girls jogged just a bit ahead, bumping shoulders the way they often did when they walked together. Apparently the earlier remark about their mom brought on some memories.

Lilly started it. "Remember that fancy crystal vase thing Dad gave her a couple years ago?"

"I remember you dropping it."

"Yeah, well, when we were in the hospital last year, waiting to see her, waiting to hear if she was all right, I kept thinking about that vase. How upset she was when I broke it. She really loved that thing. And I kept thinking how I'd have given anything not to have dropped it. Because she was so hurt and I was so scared."

"Yeah, well…I keep thinking about Easter dinner. The one where we had an Easter egg hunt in the morning?"

"We had an egg hunt every Easter, doofus."

"But I meant the dinner where she had the yellow tablecloth. And the yellow flowers. And the little yellow bunnies holding the napkins. Everything was just so. Until I threw up."

Lilly nodded. "Oh, I remember that one. You were so gross."

"Everybody jumped up and left the table. Even Grandpa was gagging. And Mom started crying."

Lilly punched her sister in the shoulder. Not hard.

"Yeah, it *was* gross. But you were sick, for Pete's sake. Not like you could help it."

"I *know* that. But when Mom was in the hospital, I kept thinking about that dinner. I didn't want that Easter to be a memory in her head, not when she was so hurt."

Rosemary glanced up at Whit. A quiet frown pleated his forehead, a sign that he was also listening.

And it was Lilly's turn to come through with some memories. "Pep, it's not like you're the only one who did stuff. Remember when we got our two-wheelers? And I fell and skinned my knee and there was blood all over the place and I ran home as fast as I could."

"And Mom had that white cloth all over the living room carpet. She was measuring something. I can't remember what."

"I don't remember, either. I just remember running toward her and blood getting all over that white material and her being so mad."

Pepper punched her sister in the shoulder. Not hard. "She never stayed mad at you for long. Remember how mad she was at *me* when I skipped school in kindergarten?"

"You were such a dolt. How could you think nobody would notice you were gone?"

"You didn't have to tell."

"I wasn't *telling*. Like tattletale. But I didn't know what happened to you!"

"You *told*. And when I got home I sneaked in the back door because I could see a police car out front. The police were there about *me*."

"How was I supposed to know that? You could have been sick or in an accident or something. When you do something dumb, you're supposed to tell me first, remember?"

"All I remember was that Mom wouldn't let me watch television for a whole year."

Lilly rolled her eyes. "It was maybe for a week. Not a year. Besides, remember the first time we went to the dentist. And you didn't want to go. And you ran out as soon as Mom opened the car door and ran right in the street and Mom had to run after you and there were cars honking all over the place—"

"I thought it was funny," Pepper insisted.

"Me, too. It *was* funny. Except to Mom."

They'd almost reached the house. The girls had slowed their pace, and Rosemary not only slowed down, but didn't want to breathe. Everything they said gave her pictures of their mom, of how their family behaved together— at least how Zoe was with her daughters.

Pepper hesitated before they got to the back door. "Mom always said I was a lot of trouble."

"Yeah, well. I wish sometimes that we could have had some do-overs."

"Me, too."

"But you didn't have to worry like I did. You were the good kid. I was the troublemaker. If anything happened, everyone looked at me first, like Mom *knew* I'd been behind it somehow."

Lilly struggled for a second before responding. "When she died, though, Pep, remember how you hit the wall? That's what I wanted to do. Hit things. Hit things hard. The way you did. I wanted to be like you lots of times. In the hospital, I was so sad I was sick. But I couldn't *do* anything."

"Hey."

Whit's quiet voice interrupted the two. Maybe he believed it was a good idea for the girls to talk, get some of those things off their chests. But when he suddenly stepped forward, Rosemary realized what had changed.

The girls had gone from talking to crying. Their faces turned toward their dad, and it got worse. Both of them erupted with tears. Snuffling, nose-dripping tears. And when Whit lifted his arms, both girls hurtled toward him, burying their faces in his chest.

Rosemary sucked in a breath. They'd reached the back door, and he motioned for her to come in with them—and that's what she'd initially planned to do. But not then. Not when the girls were upset, when the three of them were obviously having a private, fragile family moment together.

The girls and Whit had so easily made her feel part of their family group.

But at a time like this, Rosemary thought she needed to remember that she was an outsider, an interloper.

Whit protested about her leaving, but she made hearty noises about seeing them tomorrow, that she had some work she needed to do.... Aw, hell's bells, she had no idea what excuses she came up with. She just got out of there as fast as she could, with a fast kiss for each girl and a squeeze on Whit's arm for a goodbye.

Right then, that was the best she could do.

Unfortunately she was close to crying herself.

Chapter Eight

Whit put together cheese and bacon sandwiches for the girls, which had always been one of their favorites. The best he could do for a vegetable was to plaster some cream cheese in celery, which they usually liked, too. Both only picked at their food.

Truthfully, he didn't immediately notice how quiet they were at first, because he'd felt pensive ever since Rosemary left. On the walk home, when the twins started talking, he'd been startled at the words coming out of their mouths.

Whit knew his marriage to Zoe wasn't the happiest. He remembered, too well, how difficult it was to live in the pristine house she valued so much. And Zoe had been so sure that marrying a landscape architect would add up to a good life, as defined by money and status.

Whit never had a problem bringing in good money, but Zoe hadn't counted on him coming home with muddy feet and dirt under his fingernails. But the girls had seemed devoted to Zoe, and she'd been a very good mother. They'd always been dressed to the nines. They had salon haircuts. She'd made sure they had riding and dancing lessons. That was her version of being a good mom, and Whit had never been sure she was wrong.

But it hurt, this afternoon, listening to his daughters' stories. He hadn't known they experienced some of the same guilt that he had. He could never guess what wrong thing was going to offend her next. Zoe had the textbook on the "right way to live" and he'd never known the rules until he broke them. During most of the marriage, he'd simply shut up and tried to keep the peace. But he never realized that Zoe had made their daughters feel badly—for doing nothing more than being kids.

Rosemary must have formed impressions from hearing Lilly and Pepper—but he wasn't sure what she'd thought…much less why she'd taken off so abruptly.

And temporarily his concerns were tabled because the girls jumped up from the table and carried their dishes to the counter. Every alarm bell in his nerve system went off. They cleared the table, often did dishes—but only after a lot of badgering and bargaining and stalling. Their volunteering to do the chore without any prompt at all warned him that something was going on.

It got worse. After the dishes were stashed in the dishwasher, they wiped down the counters and swept the floor.

Whit wanted to search for antacids in the first aid kit, but he was afraid to leave them.

He first wanted to have an inkling of what was going

on. So he stoked the fire. Picked up a book from the floor.

"Hey, Dad." Predictably when the twins were planning Armageddon, Pepper took the lead. She and Lilly wandered over to the west window, where they could see their handmade crèche. It was dark as pitch, but their glow sticks created a soft light on the scene.

The manger definitely looked better by night than day.

"We had a good time today, didn't we?" Pepper continued. "It was like...unique. We never did anything like that before."

"I liked it, too," Whit said. "Especially liked doing it with you two."

"And Rosemary." Lilly exchanged a quick glance with Pepper. "Both of us have been worried that she was upset."

So this was the topic they'd been brewing on? "Because she left before dinner?"

"Yeah. We were thinking...maybe we shouldn't have talked about Mom so much."

"Yeah," Pepper chimed in. "I mean, she's done all this great stuff with us. And she's alone this Christmas, too. And then we started talking about Mom and feeling sad."

"Hmm," Whit said.

"What if we hurt her feelings? Like maybe she thought we weren't thinking about *her* being alone. And tomorrow's Christmas Eve. And we want her to come over on Christmas Day, too. And she said she would."

Lilly added, "Tomorrow she said we could go over to her place and make a bunch of stuff. Like a coconut cake for dessert on Christmas. And a blueberry coffee cake for Christmas morning. And like black cherry Jell-O in a mold, you know, like we both liked since probably before we were born. And she said we could have cocoa with marshmallows while we're making everything."

"But we're worried that won't happen if she's upset with us," Pepper said urgently.

"All right. I don't think that's the case, but if you're worried about, I think you should call her."

"No. We can't do it." Pepper and Lilly exchanged glances again, then looked at him. "We think the only answer that'll work is if you go over to her place, Dad."

"Me? Now?"

"Listen, Dad." Pepper pushed Lilly ahead, the way she always did when she thought Lilly could present the most persuasive argument. "First off, it's not very late. And you could talk to her the way a grown-up talks. So if we did something to upset her, you could explain it or fix it. She probably wouldn't say anything to us— not the truthful, *real* thing—because she's nice. And she wouldn't want to hurt our feelings. So if we asked her, we still might never know why she left so fast."

"And tonight, besides, Lilly and I were just gonna watch a movie. *The Hunger Games.*"

"You already saw it," Whit reminded them.

"Exactly. The first time we saw it with you. Because you said we either saw it with you or we didn't get to go. But now we've seen it, and you did, too, so you know it isn't terrible or too old for us or anything. And we want to see it again and you don't. So it's easy, you know? You can go over and talk to Rosemary, and you don't want to be here anyway while we're watching a movie you don't even like."

Whit scratched his head. He was positive a shoe was going to drop. The kids were offering him a chance to do the one thing he really wanted to do—even though they didn't know it. Surely fate was going to show up and drop a shoe on his head. This was just too easy.

"I don't like leaving you at night."

"Like you think we're babies? That's just dumb. If something happened, we could call you and you could be back here in less than ten minutes. What could happen? Even if another bear showed up, we could hide and call you. For Pete's sake, you'd just be a little way up the mountain."

Whit looked up. There had to be a cloud in this sky. There just had to be. "Well, maybe Rosemary's not up for company. For sure I should call her first—"

"No, no! No calling first! That'd just give her a chance to say she's tired or she's working. And then we still won't know if something's wrong. You have to just show up." Pepper frowned. "Like...take something. A glove. Say we thought she dropped it."

"That won't work, dolt," Lilly interrupted. "Dad can't lie. He's no good at it."

Wilt wanted to pursue that unexpected character judgment, but just then he didn't want to look a gift horse in the mouth and risk it disappearing. "Well, if you two are sure you think it's a good idea..." He said grudgingly.

"We do. We both do. And like we can call you or you can call us if there's any problem. We can't go get you. Unless you'd let me drive the Gator—"

"No."

"Worth a try," Pepper muttered to Lilly.

Whit was out the door before he let a bark of a chuckle escape. The girls were so sure they'd outwitted him.

Of course they often did outwit him. Both were smarter than he was, and together, they were formidable.

But right now there was nothing on his mind but Rosemary. All afternoon, he'd watched her with the kids. She wasn't just a natural mom; she was a natural nurturer. Full of fun. Full of zesty energy and up for anything. So easy, so natural to be with. And not just for the girls.

He'd never been comfortable with Zoe. He'd been in love with her, the way a young man could be crazy in lust, and what could possibly matter more than sex when you're a kid? Sex mattered then. And later. And probably forever, Whit figured, since he hadn't noticed any lessening in drive or need.

But the urge had paled in the past years with Zoe. She wasn't any less beautiful. Any different than she'd ever been. But he hadn't noticed, for so long, how critical she was of everyone and everything. He could go weeks without doing anything right. Weeks where he didn't want to go home—except to see the girls. Where dinner and breakfast and weekends were an effort, to be careful about what he said, what he did, how he did pretty much anything.

Rosemary was like…a fresh rose.

Complex. Way smart. But no undercurrents other than pure sweet female, a woman who loved life and loved others and loved every adventure a day could bring.

He wanted to call it smitten. Wanted to call it a major lust attack. Wanted to call it all kinds of things—because it seemed too damn soon to be so sure. But he was sure, like it or not. That he'd fallen in love with her.

Real love.

The SUV already knew its way to her house, even on a pitch-black night, on the unlit mountain road. It was only when he saw the lamp shine in a downstairs window that his stomach suddenly clutched.

Out of nowhere, he suddenly remembered that she'd left faster than a bat out of hell that afternoon. She'd been stressed. He'd guessed a zillion reasons why—starting with her being horrified at the images of Zoe she must have formed—or because the girls' crying had hit her in some unforeseen way—or, or, or. He could guess reasons forever, but the fact was…he didn't know.

And he really had no idea what kind of reception he might get when he knocked on her door.

When Rosemary left Whit and the girls, she felt as unsettled as a cat in the rain. While she put away her jacket, her gaze flew to the fragrant tree, and the crazy, wonderful decorations the girls had made for it.

Somehow the tree made her feel another naggy restlessness.

Christmas should be about kids. And family.

She felt so badly that the girls had broken down into such a serious cry fest. It wasn't that she thought crying was bad. And bringing up memories of their mom wasn't a bad thing, either. But she hadn't wanted to provoke painful memories for the kids…or for Whit.

The whole afternoon had relentlessly reminded her of what she already knew. Whit and his girls' memories of Zoe were still very much part of their lives.

As much as she cared, as much as she'd even come to love them, she was inarguably an outsider. They needed each other, needed to be with each other that night. She understood that.

But she still felt mighty lonely in the big old lodge. She wasn't up for working. Wasn't up for settling in front of a movie or TV show. She couldn't concentrate enough to read.

So…she poured a glass of wine and carted a vanilla candle upstairs to the bathroom. It wasn't often she had a total pamper session, but tonight seemed the time for it.

An hour later, she'd finished half the wine and peeled off a green facial mud mask. She stepped into the shower for the rest of the spa treatment. There wasn't much she could do with her hair, except give it an extra dose of conditioning. Then came shaving her legs— with real shaving cream, because she loved the foam.

It had been months since she'd given herself the whole female indulgence thing, and she wasn't humming by the time she stepped out of the shower and reached for a plump red towel. But she was *almost* humming.

A happier mood was trying to sneak back, and part of that was remembering some of the great things that day. How all four of them had laughed. How they'd all taken the manger idea seriously. How Whit was such a total sucker for anything that made his twins smile. How Lilly was so thoughtful and caring. How Pepper needed someone to help her believe she wasn't just a screw-up.

When it came down to what mattered…she'd laughed more in the past week than she'd laughed in months and months.

The sound of someone pounding on her front door startled her—and made her catch her breath. People occasionally got lost on the mountain…but December 23 was an unusual time for hikers and campers. She'd never been afraid up here. She'd learned young to be self-reliant, and she knew every nook and cranny of her mountaintop. Still, it was dead dark and almost nine at night.

When she failed to answer immediately, someone pounded on her door again. She grabbed jeans and a sweatshirt from her bedroom, yanked them on over still wet skin, used her fingers to comb her damp hair and yelled, "I'm coming!" when the door pounding continued.

She ran downstairs barefoot, her heart starting to pound, instinctively grabbed her gun from the closet top shelf, ran to the door, looked out…

And there was Whit.

He looked cold, his shoulders hunched, his hands stuck in a buffalo plaid shirt jacket, his head bowed. His face appeared blue-white in the yard light.

She immediately opened the door. "You didn't have to stand in the cold, you could have just come in! You know I don't lock the door!"

"I was afraid I'd scare you."

"You did. How come you didn't call first?"

"Because the girls insisted I come over without calling. I'm here on their very specific orders."

"Really," she said quietly. She was pretty sure he hadn't made up fibs before…but the way he looked at her as he pulled off his flannel jacket and tossed it on the couch had no resemblance to a mild-mannered dad. He looked like a lone wolf hungry for firelight. Hungry for her.

"They wanted me to apologize."

"For what?"

"You were terrific with them, Rosemary. The girls—and me—we couldn't have had a better afternoon. And even if it sounds odd, that includes the girls doing some crying near the end. I mean—I don't want you feeling bad about their getting a little upset. I've never been sure if they're supposed to talk about their mom all the time or not. I think it was good, their letting out those memories. And for me, it just felt better because you were there. Because—"

"Whit, it's okay to take a breath." Her tone turned gentle. She'd never seen him talk nonstop before. Never seen him remotely nervous. Once his jacket was off, his hand scraped through his hair. He pivoted around and saw that the fire needed tending, so he hunched down, opened the screen and grabbed the poker.

"They're counting on coming over here tomorrow. Apparently you offered to let them cook with you? Or bake, I guess they said. Stuff that would be part of dinner for the next day. And I forgot to ask you what time we should come for Christmas dinner, mostly because

I don't have a clue. I've got a twelve-pound ham. Not sure how long that takes to cook. I was hoping you could tell me—"

"Whit."

"They're watching one of those *Hunger Games* movies. I'm opposed to kids seeing violence and sex in movies, and even though they think they're old enough, they're only eleven. I went with them the first time, which mortified them to death—which they've told me over and over. Thank God I knew some other dads who insisted on going, too, so I wasn't the only one embarrassing my daughters into an early grave, which they still bring up at every opportunity—"

"Whit. You didn't come here for the girls."

Finally. He stopped talking. Stopped stoking the fire and adding logs and poking it and being busy. He looked at her. "What do you mean?"

"You came for me," she said softly.

"I know. I—"

"You came for me," she repeated, even more softly.

The fire cracked and popped, shooting sparks up the chimney. She flipped off the overhead light—the only glaring light in the room—and then came toward him. She saw his head tilt, expressing a question about what she was doing, but she couldn't have answered him.

She didn't know what she was doing. At least not exactly. For sure she wasn't seducing him, because George had scrubbed any aggressive sexual ideas out of her head with a Brillo pad. But Whit...

She'd seen how he looked at her.

He'd been celibate since Zoe's death—she'd have bet the farm on it.

So he had to be horny. Probably horny times a million. And the girls still dominated his heart, his emotions, so that's how it would likely be for a while yet.

But when she came close—close enough—to lift her arms around his neck, to lift up, to lift her lips to his…a low groan came out of him that was more primal than a wolf's cry.

Just like that, she knew what Whit wanted for Christmas. And that she was likely the only one who could possibly give it to him.

It was easy, so easy, to love him. The first touch of her lips and he folded faster than a house of cards. His arms roped around her, his big hands sliding around her ribs, her waist, pulling her to him. Closer. Then closer yet, until she was leaning against him, her breasts crushed against his chest, her pelvis cradled between his hips. He was erect. In those two seconds, he'd already gone harder than rock, as if she had the precise key for his ignition switch.

His mouth took her invitation and made it into a party. A private party, involving intoxicants and sweets and music and firelight. He was the intoxicant. She was his sweet taste. The fire glowed on his face, on his harshly intent expression, on his closed eyes.

Then her eyes closed, too, taking in the rush of his wanting her, of his touch, the feel of him, the warmth and power of him. The need.

Her need, too.

For so long, she'd needed…without a name for what it was. Needed a man she could trust. Needed to love. To feel loved. Needed to express….

This.

Heat like a fire.

Need like a force. Delicious need. Luxurious, wicked need. Labor intensive need.

And yeah, she worked to provoke, to incite, to please. It was hard work, touching Whit. Yanking off his henley sweater, laying her cheek against his heartbeat as she slowed down, letting her fingers tickle through chest hair, discover the slope of his chest and ribs, find the iron in his shoulders and upper arms.

She tried a kiss on his chest after that, an eyes-closed, petal-soft trail of kisses from his Adam's apple down, down...

Courage came easily. He was so responsive— the sounds he made, the way his body heated for her touch, tensed for her touch, so readily conveyed that he was starting to burn, hot and bright. Maybe he wasn't thinking about her...but for certain he wasn't thinking about Zoe and loss, about kids and loneliness, about life.

He was just...living. Not thinking, not analyzing.

He was just heart-beating alive. Heart-thundering alive.

With her. For her.

Even as those thoughts raced through her head in flashes, she was touching, stroking, learning him. A little fear seeped in there. Not fear of him. Not exactly anyway. It was just...he was so much bigger, so much stronger, so...much. The hammer in his jeans strained the zipper. Strained against her leg to free him, to un-cage the tiger.

And that was when that unexpected worried quiver showed up again. She'd never teased a tiger before.

Back when, she'd thought George was. It had been

more than startling to discover George had no more prowess than an alley cat.

And that was the thing she never let surface, didn't want to ever surface, and for damn sure, she didn't want to think about him now. But her history proved that she hadn't been enough for George. Hadn't been enough for a stupid, immoral alley cat.

So it was pretty darned hard to feel safe with a tiger.

Particularly when she abruptly found herself on her back, on the hearth rug, and the look in Whit's eyes was a whole lot hotter than the fire. "So," he said, in a slow voice as if he had all the time in the world to spend on that one syllable, "we know you're a hard-core giver."

"Not necessarily," she began, annoyed as the devil when some of those worried quivers showed up in her voice.

"Yeah. Necessarily. You're a hard-core giver all the time. And as I keep discovering, you're a relentless giver, as well."

"That's not—"

"Yeah, it is true. But the question is, the really serious question, is how good are you at taking?"

"Tak—?" She was utterly confused at the whole conversation, partly because her tongue was so thick, her mind so discombobulated, that she couldn't follow much of anything. At least anything verbal.

The kiss that leveled her flat to the ground…her entire body comprehended that right off. Whit was a bully. Who knew? There were massive holes in his character she hadn't been exposed to before. His bully side. His demanding side. His earthy, no limit to his bad ideas side. His…

She couldn't breathe.... She sucked in a lungful of oxygen when he finally lifted his mouth. His mouth was wet from hers. Bruised from hers. He wasn't breathing all that easily, either. But he looked at her hard again, with that same fire glow in his eyes.

"So...you're not just a giver. You get an A for amazing in the giving category. But we're going to have to work on the taking thing. Think selfish.

"Think greedy. Think 'I want.' Can you do that for me?"

He was talking gibberish. Not making any sense she could comprehend. But she heard the low, throaty tone in his voice. He was talking love words. He was talking coaxing. Wooing. Wanting.

And then he quit talking. Peeled off her sweatshirt, then fought and won her jeans, found bare skin.

Oh, man. He was deep trouble anywhere near bare skin. He sucked in a breath at the look of her, bare, in firelight, vulnerable like she'd never felt vulnerable. By the time he met her eyes again, she considered shrinking. All that concentrated danger in his gaze was downright scary.... At least for a woman who already knew she couldn't make a man happy, not sexually, even when she thought she was pretty naturally comfortable with herself that way. Whit was just different.

Whit was more man.

More man times a million or so.

He changed gears, from high speed to a torturous crawl. Every little thing seemed to slow him down. Her tongue, her lips, her throat. He washed her navel with his tongue, flipped her over...made an adventure trail down her spine with his kisses, took a small, careful nip of her fanny...then flipped her over again.

The man was more powerful than a Hummer. She couldn't catch her breath, couldn't think. He wasn't giving her a chance to do what she needed to do, knew how to do. She wanted to stroke him the right way, the kind of touch that made him feel wanted, desired. She wanted to remember to make the right sounds, the sounds that made a man believe she was enthralled, hot for him.

She knew what to do.

He just wouldn't give her a chance to do it.

The fire hissed and crackled. Shadows danced on the wall, a slow dance of profiles, his, hers, always in motion. A coffee table pushed away. Couch pillows scattered. The dance of fire turned into a glossy sheen on his skin...on hers.

Every nerve in her body turned tense, fraught as wire stretched too tight. All the sensations that had been deliriously, wonderfully changed. Nothing was right. Her pulse picked up edgy, restless beats. Her heart picked up an unhappy thrum. She felt a confused myriad of feelings—thrills like skydiving, wild like running naked in the rain, restless that this would never stop, never get where she needed to go.

She wanted to tell him...something...but then his greedy hands claimed another forbidden spot. The inside of her thigh, behind her knee. Then his fingers found the nest of blond hair, combed through it, found the core of her, forced her to gasp.

He took that gasp seriously. Really seriously, as if world peace were at stake. Worked at winning another gasp out of her.

Then another.

She considered pounding on his head, but he studied the expression on her face and let out a throaty chuckle. "I think one of us is ready."

"Did you get a degree in torture?"

"Thanks. I wanted to do better, but it's been a while. I'm way, way out of practice."

"Are you still talking?"

But then she couldn't talk, either. He moved his hands under her hips, pulled her legs up and around him, climbed on and then in. She sucked in her breath at the sensation of him filling her, her being stretched to the maximum. The torture he'd inflicted before was nothing like this. This was misery at the most exhilarating level, need that took her over and under. Need for him. Need for fulfillment. Need she wanted to scream for.

She didn't scream. But she called out. His name. Furiously, fiercely. Over and over. He was calling hers as well, not in a scream but in a soft, urgent hiss of a whisper. The hot, wild ride headed for a cliff, tipped over.

He collapsed on top of her, then seemed to realize that his weight could crush her and immediately flipped her on top of him. He tried collapsing again, then seemed to realize that she could be cold, so he lifted up, tugged off a throw from the couch, draped it over her, then crashed for the third time.

This time he was out for the count, breathing hard, eyes closed. Recovery wasn't about to come fast.

Recovery was never going to happen for her. Rosemary figured she wouldn't survive making love with him a second time. She was beyond sated. A stupid smile had become glued on her mouth; she still hadn't caught her breath; and her heart was still slamming like a jackhammer. If there was an earthquake, an avalanche, a tornado all at once, she still couldn't have moved. Not then.

Her skin was slick, against his sweat dampened skin. Her cheek rested right in the curve of his shoulder. Her ear pressed against the wild pulse in his throat. She felt his arm around her, his big hand still securing the blanket over her. She tried to grasp a little reality again.

Couldn't.

There was nowhere else she wanted to be than right there, hot and naked in his arms. She didn't want to think about it. Didn't need to think about it. Ten minutes from now, the world might well crash on her head. But not at this second.

Nothing was wrong. Everything was right. For the first time in months. Maybe for the first time in forever.

Days passed. Maybe months.

Maybe just minutes.

She felt the stroke of his hand, his fingers combing into her short hair. "I need to tell you something."

Instinctively she braced. "Sure."

"I meant to tell you before."

"It's all right. Just say it." Whatever it was, she was positive she wouldn't want to hear it.

"The first time I saw you, I thought you were extraordinarily beautiful. The kind of beauty that I couldn't get out of my mind. Special beautiful. Uniquely beautiful. Your heart shows up in your eyes."

"Pardon?"

"I didn't know this was going to happen. But I'd

thought about it." Again, his palm stroked her hair, her neck. "I wanted this. Wanted you. The more time I was around you, the more I was…drawn."

"You'll get over it," she assured him. "I'm feeling delusional right now, too. But then, I've never made love with that much energy. It probably blew out most of my common sense brain cells."

"You're funny. But you're still beautiful. Even if you don't want to hear it. And I'm confused."

"I know you are," she said sympathetically.

"Rosemary. You don't have to fake it. And if you felt you needed to fake it with that ex-fiancé of yours, then he had to be damned stupid and a jerk you're well rid of."

"Fake it?" Now she propped herself up on her elbows, using his chest as a table, and the look she leveled on him wasn't sweet.

"Okay. I'm sorry I brought it up. Not a time to be blunt. I've been accused before of having the finesse of a junkyard dog."

"I never faked it."

"I'm sure you didn't. I was way off base. And I shouldn't have said anything anyway."

"You're right. You shouldn't have." She repeated, "I never faked anything."

"I'd be willing to offer diamonds or rubies or a Mercedes to get out of trouble."

"And furthermore, you have plenty of finesse. Loads. Heaps."

"Um, was that a compliment or a complaint?"

"A compliment, you idiot."

He was still stroking her hair. Still looking into her eyes...as a lover. Possessively. Greedily. Intimately.

"I'm thinking this would be a great time for the phone to ring. Anything to get me out of hock until I figure out how to get my foot out of my mouth." Abruptly a cell phone went off from the pocket of his jacket across the room. "Damn. I didn't mean it. I swear."

"It could be your girls."

"It has to be my girls. At this hour. At this time of night before Christmas Eve tomorrow. Do I have to answer it?" he asked her plaintively.

"Afraid so."

"But I don't want to leave you."

A minute before he'd been so aggravating she wanted to strangle him. Then he said that, and she remembered they were both still naked, still glued together, and maybe her fresh arousal wasn't as public as his, but she wanted him again. Right then. As hard and wild and scary as the first time had been.

The cell peeled out a rap beat again. She said what he already knew. "You have to take the call."

And he uncurled and stood up to do just that, but as he connected the call and pressed the speaker button, Pepper's plaintive voice started up. "Dad. Lilly's already asleep but not me. But she was worried, too. We just wanted to be sure Rosemary wasn't mad at us."

Rosemary had to smile, both at Whit walking naked across the room to dive for his cell phone—the firelight incredibly illuminating his tight little ass. And it was little, compared to those big brawny shoulders and muscular thighs. Sexy. Head to toe.

But even more, lovably, when he scraped a hand

through his hair and talked to his daughter. "Rosemary was never mad at you. She liked it, that you were willing to talk about your mom with her." He glanced back.

She gave him an enthusiastic thumbs-up.

He turned around, so he could look at her even as he talked to his daughter. "And yeah, she's totally still on for the cooking thing tomorrow...."

She sent him another thumbs-up.

"So she wants you to come over around, say..." He waited.

She held up both hands, fingers splayed.

"Around ten o'clock, she says. So you'd better get to sleep, cookie. I'll be home in two shakes."

The instant he clicked off, he scowled and said, "I don't want to be home in two shakes."

She laughed, and draping the couch throw around her shoulders, started scooping up his clothes. He dressed. Unwillingly. Stopped to kiss her. And then return to scowling as he yanked on boots, and finally his jacket. Then kissed her again.

"So do I get to come over tomorrow or is it just the girls who get to come?"

"You can come over midafternoon. We need to do the baking stuff on our own. Unless...well...the only job we have open before midafternoon is washing dishes."

"That's just cruel," he said.

"Uh-huh." She opened the door, then wrapped the throw seriously tight around her. Outside, the night was black velvet, not a star or moon in sight—but toe-stinging cold. "Whit?"

"What?"

"I need to tell you something."

His head shot up, and his eyes lost all that teasing silly nonsense. "So tell me."

"I wanted to say it before."

His expression changed, as if he were bracing for a hurt. She'd felt the same way when he'd started a conversation with those same words. Nothing good ever seemed to follow "I need to tell you something."

She said softly, "I'm really, really glad we did this."

He waited, as if assuming an ax was going to fall on his foot after that announcement.

But there was no ax. She smiled softly, bravely. "Before you go home…I just want you to know that this whole night was absolutely okay. It's the Christmas season. Everything gets crazy emotional around the holiday—for you and the girls especially this year, because of Zoe. I never wanted to interfere with that. Never wanted any of you to think I wanted or could replace her." He opened his mouth, but she pressed two fingers—two very cold fingers now—against his lips.

"Whit, I really wanted to be here for you. I loved having the chance to be here for you. But after the holiday, I know you three are going back to Charleston. And that's fine. I don't want you to worry even a second about tonight. This was all good."

She lifted up, pressed a kiss on his lips—a fast, fast smooch—and then chuckled. "Go, would you? I need to close the door before I freeze to death."

She didn't give him a chance to answer—or a chance to think up some awkward reply. She just closed the door. Fast. Before he could see how hard it was to hold on to that soft smile.

She hustled to the warmth of the fire and crouched

down to secure the screen for the night, feeling that she needed to lock up her emotions the same way. Whit had made her feel beautiful.... When she'd never felt beautiful before.

But after the holiday, she knew he would have trouble remembering her.

Every man she'd ever known seemed to find it all too easy to forget her.

Chapter Nine

The house was quiet as a cave when Whit woke up. He pulled on clothes as he glanced outside. The moon was still up, the landscape black and glistening and silent. A perfect Christmas Eve day was dawning.

There wasn't a whisper coming from the loft—the girls were still clearly dead to the world. He measured coffee, put it on, did some token cleanups until the percolating finally finished.

He carried the mug to the tree, stared at the lopsided wonder they'd created. From the thrown cranberries to the loopy popcorn strands to the sequin slipper Pepper had donated for the top, it was the best tree he could remember.

Because of her.

Rosemary.

Heaven knew where she'd been hiding all that passion...but he'd never figured, at his age, to be blown away by making love. It was her. All her. She inspired his girls; she inspired him. That huge heart of hers seemed to have no limits. She had an endless capacity to give and understand, a magical intuition and perception about what others needed.

He thought about what she'd looked like, naked in the firelight.

He thought about her standing in the doorway, the couch throw covering her but her feet still bare, her legs, her eyes in that freezing night wind, telling him it was okay, she didn't want or expect more from him.

She had the right to expect the moon and the stars from a man. She deserved the best of guys. She deserved to be cherished and appreciated. To be loved.

And he wanted to be the guy to love her. To be loved by her.

Only they'd barely made love before she was kicking him out.

"Hey, Dad." Lilly, loudly yawning, ambled downstairs, wearing her lion floppy slippers and her Christmas jammies, her hair all atumble. "Is it time to go to Rosemary's yet?"

"It's not even eight, lovebug."

"We're gonna have a *great* day." She yawned again. He lifted an arm, and she scooched next to his side, curling up the way she had since she was a little girl. "You're bringing the ham to Rosemary's house, right?"

"Right."

"And the pop."

"And the pop."

"And the ice cream Christmas trees."

"And the trees."

"So we won't have anything to do but love Christmas."

"That's the plan I heard," Whit agreed. "I was told I couldn't come over to her house today, though, until midafternoon. Unless I was willing to shut up and do dishes all morning."

"We're doing girl talk, Dad. You'd be bored anyway. Or you'd be holding your hands over your ears so you didn't have to hear embarrassing stuff. Besides...don't you want to get something for Rosemary for Christmas?"

He hesitated. "You're right. I could pick up something this morning. Do you think it'd be a good idea if it was from all of us?"

Pepper showed up in the doorway. "I think Lilly and me should get her something that isn't, like, a *thing*. We could put a present in an envelope. Like that we'll do all the dishes tomorrow. Or we could vacuum or something. Or fold clothes. You know. Some dumb chore so she wouldn't have to do it."

Lilly considered that idea. "Yeah. That's good. She's not so much about stuff from stores. But still. We could write it on a piece of paper, and in an envelope, and then in a box, and then in a bigger box, and then wrap it up so she couldn't guess what it was."

"And Dad could get us some boxes and wrapping paper if he's going out anyway." Pepper elbowed her way to his right side, where she curled up next to him.

"I wasn't planning a long shopping trip," Whit said.

Lilly shot him a frown. "But you need to take your time, Dad. You need to get something neat for Rosemary."

"Like what do you think is a good idea?"

"I don't know. Just something special and nice and that's a good surprise for her. Like that."

Acid starting churning in his stomach. He wasn't an anxiety-ridden kind of guy, never had been. It was just…well, he'd rather wrestle with a nest of rattlers than shop for a woman. Nothing he'd ever gotten Zoe had pleased her. No matter how hard he tried. And he'd tried. "Like what kind of nice?"

"Dad." Pepper patted his shoulder. "Go to Greenville Park near downtown. Then just walk. All the shops will be open. You'll see something just right. You can do this."

"Yeah. You can do this, Dad." Lilly stepped up to reassure him, too. "Just take your cell phone. Call us if you get in trouble."

That was a big help. He was already in trouble. Trouble that had nothing to do with his girls or buying a present.

It had to do with falling in love with a woman he'd only known for a few days. A woman who seemed quite sure he was suffering from holiday madness. A woman who had a secret regarding her ex-fiancé—a secret that put sadness in her eyes, a secret that led her to hiding out as a hermit. And a woman who was under the impression that he was still in mourning for Zoe.

A few more days with her. That's all he had. All he and the girls had.

Whit could rack his brain from here to Poughkeepsie. But he had no idea how he could make all that come together in such a short time.

* * *

When Whit showed up to drop off the girls, he came to the door with them.

She greeted the crew with a big smile. "You want some coffee, Whit?" she asked, and it looked as if he was about to answer, but then he just stood there and looked at her.

And she looked back.

It happened again, just like last night. No one had ever made her feel beautiful—because she wasn't. But Whit made her feel treasured that way.

And no one had ever made her feel unforgettable— because all her life, from parents to boyfriends to George, she'd apparently been easy to forget.

Whit was the only one who evoked entirely different emotions. It was the way he looked at her. The way her life seemed different, the way she felt differently, the way the whole world suddenly, softly hushed, when he was close.

For a few seconds, anyway.

"Dad. What's wrong with you? You're looking weird."

"You're not sick, are you? Because it's Christmas Eve."

"And you're supposed to leave so we can bake stuff with Rosemary."

"So you need to go, Dad."

Whit fought to get a word in. To her. "I'm feeling extremely unwanted."

He shouldn't. She could have thrown herself at him right then and there. "Something tells me you'll survive a few hours of peace and quiet."

"*Go,* Dad," Pepper said with an eleven-year-old's complete lack of interest in his feelings.

"Yeah. We love you, Dad. But go." Lilly swooped up to give him a kiss, then pelted into the living room.

Shoes tumbled near the doorway. Hot pink jackets hurled onto chairs. Scarves snaked en route to the kitchen. Whit shook his head. "You sure you're up for this?"

"You'll come back to save me, won't you?"

"You know I will."

She didn't know any such thing. Growing up, she'd never expected to be saved. As an adult, she'd saved herself. She was no fragile princess, and she never wanted to be...but somehow Whit's words sent a silver tingle up her spine.

Even her most fragile orchids found a way to survive in the wild. She never thought of herself as fragile... but she did think of herself as a survivor. She always had been.

Now, though, watching him drive off in his SUV, she didn't feel so tough. She wasn't sure if anything could be right after he was gone.

"Rosemary!"

"I'm coming, I'm coming. And I hope you guys are ready to make a huge mess, because we're about to take out the whole darn kitchen."

"I'm *always* ready to make messes," Pepper promised.

"The first part of this is just to make a plain old white cake. That's easy enough...you two can take that on, right?"

"Yeah. We know how to do cakes. I do the measuring," Lilly said, "and Pepper does the mixing. And we both get a beater to lick. And we usually fight over the bowl, but you can have the bowl this time."

Rosemary chuckled. "I can see where your priorities are. Licking the batter is more important than the finished result." She'd already gotten out bowls and pans and measuring devices. "I don't know where this recipe came from. It just always seemed passed on in the family. We've been doing it so long I could probably do it in my sleep...but it'll be a lot more fun with you two."

It was. Licking the cake batter was all good. Then, when the cake came out and while it was still warm, both girls poked holes in the top of a cake with a fork. Rosemary mixed the cream of coconut with the condensed milk and poured it over the whole cake. "We'll make the frosting in a little bit, but first the cake has to cool. So we're moving on to the Christmas coffee cake."

That recipe was more complicated, including butter and sugar and eggs and orange juice and vanilla and blueberry pie filling and cinnamon and a bunch of other magic ingredients. In no time, the counters were crammed with dripping measuring devices and spoons and various size bowls.

"Wow, Rosemary. You really can make a mess."

"Thank you. That's the nicest thing anyone's said to me in a long time."

The girls giggled.

"Hey, you two. Do you have some grandmas and grandpas? Where are they? Do you ever spend holidays with them?"

'Well," Pepper said, "on Mom's side, she was an only child. That's why she was spoiled, she was always tell-

ing us. And she liked being spoiled. Anyway, Grandfather died when I was just a kid."

"I was just a kid, too," Lilly reminded her, in the tone
of the long-suffering.

"Anyway, we didn't know him much. But Grandmother used to be with us all the time. She lived in
Charleston, too. But something happened to her. We
weren't supposed to know, but Mom was on the phone
all the time because there were so many calls about
Grandma."

"She walked downtown in Charleston without her
clothes on in the middle of the night," Pepper piped
in. "And that was the end. She had to go to this place."

"I heard Mom tell Dad that Grandmother was too
young to have Alzheimer's. But I guess some people
get it younger. Anyway, we have to go see her every
once in a while." Lilly added honestly, "It's not like we
don't love her. But she's not like herself anymore. And
the whole place is scary."

"Scary how?" Rosemary asked.

"Well, she doesn't know us. At all. Or Dad. Or anyone else. Like she was knitting this sweater, only it
wasn't a sweater. It just kept getting longer and longer
until it was taller than Dad. She didn't know."

"And she'd start singing all of a sudden."

"And she said the f-word. You have to understand,
Grandmother would never, ever, *ever* say the f-word.
Or use any other bad language. So it's like she's not re-
ally our grandmother anymore."

"Dad said we have to visit her sometimes anyway. So
we do," Lilly said. "I'm just saying, we both get creeped

out when we go there." She raised suddenly stricken eyes. "Does that sound mean, Rosemary?"

"I think it sounds honest. You already know she can't help what's happening to her. It's sad." Rosemary aimed for a more cheerful note. "So how about your dad's mom and dad?"

"Oh, they're *awesome.* They just don't live here. They live around Seattle. They fly to see us a couple times a year. And Dad lets us fly there a couple times of year. Gramps is cool. He has horses and everything, lets us ride whenever we want. And Gram does pet therapy stuff. Like she raises dogs and cats—and sometimes the horses—to help out kids. Not sick kids. More like kids in trouble with the law. Tough kids who are always in trouble. But...oh, no. Oh, no, oh, no. Rosemary, I'm *so* sorry!"

Rosemary saw the pan slipping. Lilly had just poured the pie filling on top of the batter. The whole messy recipe was almost done—but neither girl could stand still for long; they had too much energy. The pan slipped when Pepper darted toward the sink...and down it went, with a crash and a spatter, upside down on the kitchen floor.

To Rosemary's shock, Pepper burst into tears...and Lilly looked ready to. Both lifted stricken faces to her. Both looked more upset than if they'd just lost a best friend.

"Good grief. What's all this? It's just a spill, you guys. So it's a pain to clean up, but that's all. It's nothing to be upset about. Pepper..." She crouched on the floor where Pepper had sunk down. "Honey, there's no reason to cry."

"There is. I ruined it."

"Well, yeah, I don't suspect we'll be able to eat it off the floor. But I'm pretty sure I've got the ingredients to make another one. Or we'll make something else."

"I still ruined Christmas Eve. I always ruin things. I was trying to do everything right. And now I broke the dish and made a mess and—"

"Honey, the glass dish is just a glass dish. Next time I'm there, I'll get a new one at Walmart."

Pepper hiccupped. "It's not like your greatgrandma's or something like that? Like an heirloom or like it cost a zillion dollars or couldn't be replaced?"

Rosemary frowned, disbelieving Pepper's tears and fears both. "Pepper. Lilly. To begin with, this is a cottage. It's a place for people to put their feet up, relax, enjoy nature and life and people and family. There's no dish or plate here that's expensive. Never will be."

"You're positive?" Pepper lifted her face for a second time to have her tears mopped up by Rosemary.

"Absolutely. I'm also positive that I don't even want to own things that I have to worry about. So this is just a big old nothing. Except for cleaning it up. We have to do that."

"I'll do it all," Pepper said immediately.

"That sounds good." Lilly had long quit looking so fearful, although she'd sat down on the kitchen floor with the other two.

"Nah," Rosemary said. "If we all help, the mess'll be cleared away in two shakes."

"That's what Dad always says. Two shakes. He means really fast."

"All right, then." Rosemary looked at both of them,

wondering who was more shook up, her or the girls. The burst of tears had seemed to come from nowhere. So had…fear. "Look. How about a hug to get us all back on track again?"

They glommed on to her faster than spit on an envelope. She'd seen Whit hug them. Hugs were so clearly part of their lives…and part of hers. Her brothers were major rib-busters, especially with her. But this was different. This was two eleven-year-old girls who flew into her arms and took her unconditional loving hug for granted—and offered the same kind back to her.

Hell's bells, the two of them almost brought tears to her eyes.

The mess was cleaned up—or cleaned up good enough. A new coffee cake was made. About then, they claimed they were starving for lunch, and because Rosemary hadn't completely forgotten about being a kid, she made mac and cheese—with extra cheese and French-fried onions.

Whit would likely show up at any time, but he wasn't here yet. "Okay, guys, the last thing we need to do is set the table for tomorrow."

Truthfully she'd never planned any such thing, but after the tear burst, she wanted to do something to boost Pepper's confidence. And Lilly's, too.

It was easy to see she'd made a good choice when the girls immediately shared worried glances.

"Here's the thing," she said calmly. "I'll finish cleaning up the kitchen. You two take charge of the table. We need the obvious—five of everything, plates, silverware, napkins, dessert plates. Oh, and glasses. Sound easy so far?"

"Is any of that good stuff?" Lilly asked bravely. "I mean, I know you said you don't have stuff that can't be replaced. But all the same, if we dropped, say, a glass, would it cost a whole lot?"

"Nope. Not that I'd care if you did. Putting out the dishes is the boring part, anyway. There's a linen closet—I'll show you where. There should be a bunch of holiday place mats. Pick out whatever you like."

"You mean, no matter what's there?"

"Yup. There's no fancy white linen in there...not for that old oak table. But there should be lots of place mats. And then in the middle of the table, we need some kind of decoration."

"Like what?" Pepper said warily.

"Well...I'll give you a bunch of things. Pine boughs. Red ribbon. A strip of red plaid fabric. The oranges poked with cloves. Some old, old salt cellars...that you might fill with almond or vanilla or cinnamon. Whatever you think would smell Christmasy. Just play with it, you know? And you can add anything you can think of."

"Like some pine cones from outside?" Lilly asked.

"Exactly. You're getting the picture. Whatever you two think would look nice. Or fun. Or pretty. Or whatever else rings your chimes."

You'd think she'd given them gold. Pepper dealt out the plates faster than a deck of cards. Lilly set the silverware and napkins just so. Then came the table decoration...and they fussed for more than a half hour, with ribbon and sprigs of pine and salt cellars they filled with spices. Then they took a look, and started all over.

Pepper came first into the kitchen. "Do you have any

marshmallows? Big's better but even little marshmallows would be okay."

"I think so. Let me look."

After that, Lilly asked for toothpicks…and peppercorns. Then they fussed with the table all over again. Lilly climbed on the table in her stocking feet, and used ribbon to tie a handful of the clove-studded oranges from the wagon chandelier.

A bunch of the marshmallows disappeared—Rosemary expected they went directly inside tummies—but the rest were turned into toothpick snowmen with peppercorns for eyes. Lilly was still fussing when Pepper, finally bored, ambled into the kitchen and plopped on a stool.

"This was way fun," she told Rosemary.

"For me, too. You thirsty?"

"Yeah. Dying of thirst."

"Cider?" Lilly wanted some, too, but she wasn't finished with her Christmas table centerpiece. Pepper hung in the kitchen, sipping cider, not saying anything…but there was something in her eyes that Rosemary noticed.

"My dad's due pretty soon, isn't he?"

"Actually, he's overdue. But I think he was afraid of getting stuck with dishes, so he might be deliberately a little on the late side."

She thought Pepper might laugh, but she just propped her elbows on the counter and hooked her chin in her palm. "Rosemary?"

"What, hon?" She tried to make her voice casual.

"Sometimes it really bothers me. That most of my memories of my mom are of her yelling at me. It's not that we didn't have good times, but most of the great times I remember were all with my dad."

Rosemary didn't know what to say or how to react. "Maybe your mom tended to yell when she was under a lot of stress?"

"But she didn't yell at Lilly that I can remember. I think sometimes…" Pepper said hesitantly, "that Mom didn't like me."

Cripes. The kid was breaking her heart. "You know what?" Rosemary said, but the phrase was just a stall.

"What?"

Rosemary gulped. "I think, maybe, that parents try so hard to make their kids safe, to teach them lessons and values that will help them in life. So sometimes it could seem like they're yelling too much. Or being mean. Or being critical. When all they're trying to do is be good parents."

Pepper stewed on that for a while. "So. Did your parents yell at you?"

"My parents weren't around enough to do much yelling," Rosemary said honestly.

"Well, I wish my mom had been more like you," Pepper said, and looked as if she was about to say something else, when Lilly yelled from the other room.

"Dad's back! He's just driving up!"

When Pepper took off for the front door, Rosemary let out a long, uneasy breath. Pepper's words punched every worry button. She never wanted the girls to think she could replace their mom—or that she wanted to take their mother's place.

She just never dreamed that either of the girls could form an attachment to her so quickly.

Or that she could feel a deep love for both of them, just as fast.

The icing on the worry was Whit. They'd made extraordinary love last night. But to presume that intimacy meant love or potential commitment or a future together was downright crazy. And unfair. To him. To his daughters.

Whatever they did together was about Christmas. Nothing else. Just Christmas. She damn well better keep that in mind.

And then she heard his voice in the living room, and felt her heart thump like a foolish puppy dog's tail.

Chapter Ten

Whit pushed off his boots at the door, then shed his jacket. His daughters gamboled toward him as if he were their favorite horse and they could both climb on.

"Where have you *been,* Dad!"

"Hey. You two sent me out with a job to do. It took a while. I'm exhausted."

Both girls giggled. "Dad, when you have to shop, you're exhausted before you even walk in the first store."

The twins couldn't be more bright-eyed and happy, but right off, he could see Rosemary was avoiding his eyes. His naked tigress from last night had disappeared. Her red sweatshirt was Christmasy; her socks had Santas. But she was hanging back in the doorway, her posture careful.

"Wow. Looks like you three have been busy." He said, looking at the pretty table.

"You think? Rosemary let us do it. Make up our own centerpiece and all." Lilly swallowed a gulp. "It wasn't like Mom would have done it—"

"It's terrific. Really pretty." Whit squeezed his daughter's shoulders. "You've got a great eye for balance."

"You think so?"

"I think so, too," Rosemary said immediately. "The girls have been going nonstop. Ask them. I've been working them both to the bone."

"No, she hasn't!" Pepper immediately defended her. "We made coconut cake for dessert tomorrow. And a fancy coffee cake for tomorrow morning."

"As you can tell," Rosemary deadpanned, "we concentrated only on the important food groups."

"I figured that ahead of time. The list you gave me was for all the dull stuff—like the twelve-pound ham in the back of the car."

"Which you get to stud with more cloves, Dad!"

"Not that! Anything but that!"

"And tomorrow," Rosemary added, "if you're really, really good, we'll let you peel potatoes."

Whit looked at his daughters. "I thought you guys loved me."

"We do love you, Dad," Lilly assured him. "But you have to face it. You're outnumbered."

"But I was counting on being popular when I got back. I brought dinner. And candied apples for dessert. And two DVDs to watch. And the ham. And potatoes. And..."

"All right, all right." Rosemary turned to the girls. "We did give him the grunt work. And now he's brought dinner. I think we should let him off the hook. In fact, I think we probably have to give him hero status."

Pepper and Lilly both claimed he needed more time to prove himself. "For one thing," Pepper said, "he hasn't told us what DVDs he brought yet."

"One's *Father Goose*."

"*Yeah!* That's tradition in our family, Rosemary. We always get to watch it over Christmas sometime. It's really old, but it's still pretty awesome."

Lilly wasn't giving up so easily. "What's the other tape?"

"It's a surprise. But it has *'Wedding'* in the title," Whit said, in the tone of the long suffering. As far as he knew, the girls' top ten favorite movies all had to do with brides and bridesmaids and junk like that.

Since they both screamed, he figured he'd scored a good one, but Lilly was quick to move on. "Did you get the other thing we talked about?"

"Yeah, did you, Dad?" Both girls looked at Rosemary.

They were about as subtle as a cattle prod. Rosemary picked up the hint in less than two shakes. "If you got me a present," she told him, "you can just take it right back. I haven't been out. Haven't gotten any of you three presents. You'd make me miserable if you gave me something and I had nothing to give back."

"It's not that kind of gift," Whit promised her, and to his daughters, "we're going to have to take some lessons on how to keep secrets."

Rosemary ambled closer, crossing her arms under her chest. "Listen, you three." She took a breath. "I have an idea. I think it's probably a stupid idea, and there's no problem if any of you say no."

"What? What?" The girls couldn't wait to hear.

"Well...you all came up to Whisper Mountain to have a different kind of Christmas. That's why I'm here, too. And since we've been doing things all day, and it's already almost dark...well, Christmas Eve can be on the lonely side if you're remembering the people who aren't with you. So, maybe...would you all like to sleep over?"

Whit's jaw almost dropped. His lady appeared as wary of looking at him, wary of being close to him, as a fragile doe. But before any of them could answer, she forged on.

"We've already collected all the food here. And there are a half-dozen bedrooms upstairs—you girls could either choose your own or share together. Your dad could pick another, or else sleep down here. I'm just saying, there's lots of choices, lots of ways for everyone to be comfortable."

The girls were all for it, judging from their jumping and hand slapping exuberance. So was he—but Rosemary still hadn't made eye contact with him.

He most definitely hadn't taken his eyes off of her. "I think the idea's brilliant," Whit said.

"It's probably not convenient."

"It couldn't be more convenient. Like you said, the food's already here for tomorrow. And we're not doing the usual Christmas morning big-present thing."

"I understand that...but you three probably want some family time just for yourselves. I don't want to intrude. In fact, that may be just what all three of you really want, a quiet family Christmas."

"Rosemary." Lilly's voice went up three octaves. "You're being *silly*. We're already family. We're together all the *time*."

"Yeah. We get family time whenever we want it."

"I'm on the girls' side," Whit said meekly—since the girls were already laying on the arguments.

"Well, you girls don't have nightgowns and all that—"

"It'll take me less than ten minutes to head back down the mountain, pick up a few things, get back."

She started to make another objection, then stopped. She looked at him, eyes full of worry and nerves. When he first saw those soft blues, he'd been stunned by the sadness in them. Now...some impulse had encouraged her to suggest the sleepover. Knowing her better now, he suspected she wanted to do something for the girls— some way to make Christmas Eve and Christmas morning less sad for them.

A sleepover would definitely help that. No question the girls loved the idea, and it'd be good for them. Good for him. But not, Whit suspected, so good for her, not if she was trying to back away from intimacy between them.

So he'd just have to find a way to make the sleepover a good thing for her.

Sometimes a man had to do what a man had to do.

Just after eleven that night, Rosemary opened her bedroom door and listened. Like the infamous poem claimed, not a creature was stirring, not even a mouse. The whole household had started yawning after nine, and completely folded around ten-thirty.

Rosemary knew she wouldn't sleep, so there was no point in tossing and turning. She crept downstairs barefoot, leaving lights off until she reached the far hall closet in the back.

Her mood was more than ebullient. She'd known the sleepover idea could turn out disastrous, the instant the suggestion came out of her mouth. Encouraging more closeness was risky and foolhardy—especially for a vulnerable family like those three.

But it had all gone so great. Whit made a fast trip back to their place for night gear—and came back with such a huge load that Rosemary had to hold her stomach from laughing so hard. He just looked so beleaguered as he carted in more and more stuff. The girls could have lived for six months in Europe on the "critical things" they needed to stay overnight. Their own pillows. Their own blankets. Their own "sleeping socks." And both of them claimed to have given up dolls "*ages* ago," but it seemed they both slept with life-size stuffed animals—a lion for Lilly, a panda bear for Pepper.

They all chowed down on the chili Whit had brought for dinner, adding cheese on top and dollops of sour cream, then consuming candied apples as if they'd never tasted sweets before. Then the girls charged off for their "blankies," which were apparently required before curling up with the DVDs Whit had brought.

She'd sat on one end of the couch, with the girls in between and Whit on the far end. Everyone had "blankies" heaped over them, and popcorn bowls on top of that.

Whit kept it together until halfway through *Father Goose*...when she suddenly realized he'd leaned his head back and was looking at her. If she leaned her head back, she could see him over the girls' heads. He made gestures of extreme suffering, of major yawns, of gruesome boredom, then covered his head with the blanket.

Silly. Who would have guessed Whit could be downright silly? And since she couldn't help laughing, she had to cover her head with a blanket, too. Chuckling—downright giggling—until the girls admonished the adults to behave themselves.

Rosemary was still smiling at how easily the evening had gone—and how much simple fun she'd had with them. Now, though, since she was stuck with insomnia, she pulled a footstool into the hall closet. Two weeks ago, she'd planned to forget about Christmas altogether. But now, Whit and the girls had put her in the spirit, in spite of herself.

She tugged down two boxes—neither heavy—and carted them into the living room. Family holidays hadn't always been spent at the lodge, especially not in recent years, but certain decorations had always been stored here. One box held coils of old-fashioned Christmas lights, the kind that looked like candles and clasped onto each branch.

The second box held four very old, giant glass bulbs—one sapphire, one emerald, one gold and the last ruby-red. Every generation of MacKinnon kids had to wait until they were old enough to be trusted with the "sacred" balls.

She lit candles on the mantel, providing just enough light for her to add those decorations to the tree. It didn't take long, and once she'd plugged in the old-fashioned lights, she sank in front of the tree with a blanket draped around her.

Memories whispered through her mind…so many Christmas Eves, just like this. Creeping downstairs to look at the lit-up tree, to hear the hiss of fire, to look out at winter stars, to smell the pine and cherrywood. To just inhale the magic of the night.

She heard a quiet footfall, and turned her head.

Whit, wearing jeans and a fisherman's sweater, was just coming down the stairs. "You couldn't sleep, either?"

"Just had some last-minute things I wanted to do." She noted the boxes in his hands. "You, too?"

"Yeah. The girls think we're not doing presents. And in principle, I don't think it'd kill any of us to have a less material Christmas. I know we bought all that stuff for their bedrooms at home, but that was different. And it's nothing I could wrap up, besides. Anyway…"

He was nattering. Whit was so not a natterer.

"Anyway, I bought them each a gift. A camera. Not too easy, not too complex, or that was the goal when I picked them out."

"They'll love it!"

He nodded. "I hope so. When they were talking about your darkroom, it made the mental wheels spin. They were both entranced. Pepper, I suspect, will want to take people pictures. Lilly will want to go prowl around outside, snap flowers and trees and just things that draw her eye."

"They're both artistic in different ways."

"I think so, too. When they were little, the 'twins thing' was fun for them—dressing alike, talking alike.

But these days I can see them trying to differentiate from each other. So I may have bought them both cameras, but I was hoping it was the nature of gift that they could use to develop something in their own individual style."

"And what's the third gift you just snuck under the tree?"

She caught his grin by firelight. "The nongift for you. Nothing scary. Nothing over the top. Nothing to fret about. Besides which, the kids' mother could have told you, I pretty much never get girl gifts right."

He plunked down next to her, cocked up a leg at the base of the tree. She could feel the heat of his body, see the kindling warmth in his eyes.

Too close. She said quickly, "Would you like a glass of wine? Or a beer?"

"Either one. Whatever you have around."

"I can guarantee I don't have anything fancy."

"Anything you have would be perfect," he said.

But the way he looked at her, he wasn't talking about wine. She uncoiled and aimed for the kitchen, unsure what she'd find. She had an occasional glass of wine, but living alone, a bottle usually turned to vinegar before she could finish it. Still, the lodge had a small wine keeper, just underground, with a mishmash variety of wines people had either liked or left or been gifted in the past. She found a Shiraz, opened it, poured it in two jelly glasses. Her mind whirled a million miles an hour at the same time.

There was a background reason she'd come up with the sleepover idea. The reason was real. But now she had the opportunity to do something about it...well, she sure wanted that glass of wine first.

When she came back, Whit had stoked the fire, added a log and was back on the blanket by the tree, an elbow cocked on his knee.

"That tree looks downright magical. In spite of impossible odds," he said wryly.

She handed him his wine, took a couple serious sips. "All trees look magical on Christmas Eve." She gulped. "Whit?"

He looked at her.

"I would like to tell you something—the reason I broke up with my fiancé. And the reason I've been keeping it a secret."

"I've wondered," he admitted.

She nodded. "Actually, I'd like your opinion. It was never that I was unwilling to talk about this. It was that I believed I had to keep the secret from my family. And after I tell you, maybe you could tell me if my judgment was right to keep it all quiet."

He waited. She sipped some more wine, and then started telling the story.

"I practically grew up with George, even though he was a few years older than me. His parents and mine were all doctors. The adults became close friends, did dinners together, parties, sometimes holidays. I didn't think of George—romantically—until after college. He was a brand-new doctor at the time. I was just starting my first serious job. We were both home after being away for a while, both single." She shrugged. "We started going out. Had fun. We already shared a lot of history. We didn't have to waste time getting to know each other, never suffered from those dating nerves. He was so easy to be with…it was almost like we were already family."

She had to stop for breath—and to finish the last sips of wine. "When he got me the ring, our parents were overjoyed. Beyond overjoyed. They considered it a match of the families. Perfect for everyone. To a point, I felt kind of sucked along by the tide. I loved him. It wasn't such an exciting kind of being in love, but I thought we were solid." Again, she had to stop for a gulp of breath. "Unfortunately, that's when the story gets diccy, so it gets a little tough to tell."

Whit, as if he already guessed that, had shot to his feet and made the trek to the kitchen to bring back the wine bottle. He refilled her glass.

"Well…I went to my doc for a physical. The thing was, if we were going to be married, I wanted the pill or some kind of regular birth control that we could count on. Not that I didn't want kids. I absolutely did. But I just wanted to set up house, get settled in our lives first. But the point is…in that physical, I found out that I was likely to be infertile. Skinny tubes. Wouldn't be impossible, but it was highly, highly unlikely."

"I'm sorry, Rosemary." His rough hand cuffed her neck in a quiet gesture of empathy.

"Yeah, I was, too. Devastated, to be honest. I love kids."

"You don't need to tell me that. I can see it every time you're around my girls."

"Anyway…obviously I had to tell George. Immediately, before the wedding. I didn't know if it could be a marriage stopper for him, but no matter what, I needed to get this out front for both our sakes. I thought he'd be as devastated as I was."

Whit frowned. "Instead...what? It didn't bother him?"

"At first...well, I thought he was amazingly sympathetic. Unselfish. He said he was upset, but he didn't seem to be. And then...for days after that, he kept saying things...like that this could be a cloud with a silver lining. If we couldn't have kids, we could have more freedom. Freedom to travel. To be spontaneous. To go places and do things we'd never done before. To be adventurous. To experiment in whatever we wanted to try in our lifestyles. I thought—he was trying to be kind, to help me see that we could have a good marriage without kids."

Whit's frown became darker. He didn't get it yet. Well, it had sure taken her a blue moon to get it herself. She swallowed. Hard. "Okay, so then a couple weeks before the wedding, he called, said he had a surprise for our usual Friday night date. And there certainly was a surprise waiting for me at his place. Whit, I wish to bits you could guess what it was, because I for sure don't want to tell the rest of this story."

"I'm sorry. I can't guess. And you can't keep me hanging, so just get it out."

That's what she figured she had to do. It just wasn't easy. "There was another couple at his place. A married couple. About our age, maybe a few years older. I thought he was introducing me to friends. But they weren't friends. He'd only met them once before. They were, um, partiers."

"Partiers?"

"You know. Like when four people play poker, using stakes like taking off clothes, or anteing up for some type of…behavior. They wanted to strip. To share each other. Switch off. Girls and girls. Boys and boys. Two boys and a girl. And then—"

"Rosemary, tell me you're kidding."

"I wish." She swallowed two huge gulps of wine. "Call me naive. I guess I was. And honestly, I'm not one to judge other people's choices. It's just that I never guessed in a million years that George had that kind of secret life. And there was just no chance in the universe that I wanted a marriage on those terms."

Whit crashed on his back, put a hand over his eyes. "It's hard to admit this," he said, "but the last time I was this shocked, my dad told me once and for all that a baby didn't come out of his mom's belly button."

Her jaw dropped. She didn't know how she'd expected Whit to react. She just knew she needed the story out in the open. But to hear him make a joke… she hadn't known her shoulders were stiff with tension, until all those knots loosened up. Even her face had felt stiff, because when a bubble of a laugh came out, it sounded downright rusty. "Whit."

"I can't talk now. I'm suffering too much shock."

"You goof. I'm glad I told you. You made it easy. You can't imagine…"

"Oh, yeah, I can imagine. The scene with the other couple. The scene when you told your parents the marriage was off. I'm sure glad it was you, because—even being a guy—I'd have collapsed for sure."

Another bubble of laughter escaped her. "It was so awful."

"*Awful* is too light a word. How about mortifying and upsetting and maybe even a little sickening?"

"Hey, could I hire you to be my support person?" she asked wryly.

"Sure. I'm pretty expensive. But not for you. For you, I'll do it for free."

She sank on the blanket next to him. Once the rest of the tension eased from her system, she felt as strong as a cooked noodle. "Telling George to take a hike wasn't that hard. But when it came to calling off the wedding, talking to my parents, my brothers…and his mother, who came over demanding an exact explanation." She lifted a hand in a helpless gesture. "Whit, I *couldn't* tell them. It would have affected their friendships. It was George's business, but all the parents had professional and personal connections together, thirty years of caring about each other."

"So you didn't tell. You just broke off the engagement and took off for the hills."

"Yup. You think it was cowardly?"

"I think it was damned cowardly for your ex to leave you holding the whole bag. He could have tried talking it out, finding something that both of you could say to family and friends about why the marriage was off. It shouldn't all have been on you."

"I meant, do you think I was cowardly to take off for the hills, as you put it?"

"You? Cowardly? In what universe? You take on bears and twins. You don't have a cowardly bone in your whole body."

"Yes I do."

"Where? Show me."

"Show you what?"

"Show me this cowardly bone."

Chapter Eleven

She clearly assumed he was teasing, about finding her cowardly bone.

But she went along with it, lifting her hand to the firelight, motioning to a specific bone.

"I'm pretty sure I have a lot of cowardly bones, but this has to be one of them," she said deadpan.

"Yeah?" He lifted the hand, examined it, then raised it to his mouth, pressed a soft, soft kiss in her palm.

Clearly startled, she lifted her head. Something had changed. He wasn't sure what…maybe letting the George story loose had eased her fears? Maybe he couldn't be sure of the reason, but the expression on her face was different. Unguarded. Vulnerable. And the way she looked at him was heartrending. Her eyes took him in, as if he were magic for her.

That suited him fine, because Rosemary was definitely magic for him.

He leaned closer, scooping her closer, kissing the palm of her hand again. Then looping her hand around his neck and honing down for another kind of kiss. A lip-lock. A serious mouth-to-mouth resuscitation. A kiss of wooing. A kiss of promise.

He wanted his mind and heart on nothing but her. Still, it took a second before he could completely shake off the story about her ex-fiancé. Life didn't hand out treasures very often. Rosemary was a gift, and if George was too stupid to see it, he was a fool. But he'd hurt her. And trapped her from being able to tell anyone. And in general behaved like lowdown pond scum.

For Whit, the story added even more momentum... to cherish Rosemary. To lavish her with some plain old adoring. She was so beautiful, inside and out—a woman to revere, not a woman to take advantage of. A woman to respect, not a woman who was expendable.

Convenient? No. Easy? No. Simple? No chance of that, either.

He didn't care.

He helped her sweatshirt come off— because he could see she was getting overwarm, beads forming on her forehead. Her eyes looked increasingly dazed.

His weren't. He felt he was seeing more clearly than he ever had in his life. This was the woman he wished he'd known first. Before Zoe. Before anyone else.

Her jeans had to come off, then. There was still far too much fabric separating them. He found the waist button, fought with it, won, found the zipper, eased a hand inside.

Her eyes popped open. "We can't," she whispered.

"The girls are sleeping like rocks."

"They could still wake up," she objected, but then she looked at the expression on his face and perched up on a bare elbow. "Okay, you. I have a place."

"Not outside. I'd love to make love with you outside, but right now it's colder than—"

"Not outside."

"Storm cellar?"

Better than that."

"Attic?"

"Better than that. My darkroom. It locks automatically. If the girls came to find us, they could knock, but they wouldn't be able to come in unless or until we—"

"Got it. Perfect."

He had to admit that wasn't his first impression of the room. The space was cluttered from ceiling to floor, full of odd smells and strange shapes, with very little space to maneuver. For darn sure, there was no place to lay down. But that was what he saw when she opened the door and switched on the overhead.

He realized exactly how perfect the room was when she closed the door and all light immediately disappeared.

The space was black as pitch. No way to see anything. No way to see her. But his sense of touch and hearing became fiercely acute.

"The office chair," she whispered. "It swivels and it's strong. And it might be miserably uncomfortable, but I just can't think of another place where—"

"It's perfect," he assured her. And then quit talking.

He heard her pull off her jeans...the whisk of denim, the wink of sound when she tossed them on the floor.

He listened to every sound she made—at the same

time he swiftly peeled off everything he had on. Undressing had never before involved so much adventure or risk. He bumped a shin. An elbow. A shoulder. Partly from speed, and partly because it was tough to maneuver in the small space, much less in the dark.

But he liked the dark. It made inhibitions evaporate. Intensified the other senses. It created a world where only she existed for him. Her breath. Her body. Her sounds. Her scent.

Her.

"Whit..." She was laughing. Or almost laughing. "We're going to kill ourselves."

"Yeah. It's not looking good for our surviving this. But look on the bright side...we'll have a whole lot of fun en route."

She chuckled again, the sound throaty and wicked. He loved his sunlit Rosemary...but he loved bringing out the closet wicked in her, too. "I'm just a little worried this isn't possible."

"Aw, love. You can't issue a challenge like that to a man." He heard her suck in a startled breath, grinned in the darkness. "See? Amazing what's possible when there's motivation."

He'd only gotten one good look at her working chair, but it was one of those mesh things with lumbar support and five castered feet and arm wings. There was ample room for him to sit, even to spread his legs. And it wasn't hard to lift her on his lap—he had the shoulders and muscle to do that with no sweat.

Still. Just that fast, her softest, most erotic parts shifted against his helplessly susceptible guy parts. His hands suddenly felt too rough, too harsh, for her beautiful soft flesh. And there was no possible place to put her legs, except up and over the chair arms.

And that was problematic at an Armageddon scale, because their closeness was kin to a lock and its key. One wrong move and he'd be inside her. One right move and he'd be inside her.

Either way, he had to conjure up control from somewhere or this was going to be over before it started.

And that just couldn't be.

He framed her face in his hands, pulled her closer to him for another kiss. A kiss unlike any they'd shared before. A kiss so new that no one had ever experienced it before. A kiss he created just for her. Just with her. Lips and teeth and tongues, soft and deep, owning deep, claiming deep.

She was precious. From breast to elbow, from throat to ribs, from behind her ear to the ripe swell of her breasts...there was no other woman remotely like her. Ever. Perfect for him. Part of that was her loving character and part was her inner sweetness. Part was her strength. She didn't shrink from anything, just did what was right on her own terms, alone, not expecting or asking for anything from anyone.

He didn't care if she asked for it.

He still wanted to give her the moon and the stars. To show her she was cherished. And yeah, that she was wanted. Fiercely, passionately desired. For herself. For who she was and who she wasn't.

It was a lot to tell her without saying a word. It was a lot to show her in a crowded office chair in a velvet-black room. It was a lot to comprehend, for a man who'd never felt those things, showed those things, imagined he was capable of those things.

She moaned and sighed, at first luxurious female sounds, like a cat with a nonstop purr…a sensuous, sensual kitten, responding to every stroke, every caress.

But then she got impatient. At least he thought she was impatient, judging by the small sharp teeth she dug in his shoulder—which was the precise moment he held her fanny in his hands, was holding her, steadying her, as he filled her up. He closed his eyes from the hot blood roaring in his veins, the pain of entering something so sweet, so tight, so silken.

The purrs turned into something louder. The bite in his shoulder turned into two. Good thing she didn't have nails, because her arms swung around his neck, hands, fingers digging into his skin. Sounds turned into groans. The kitten had turned into a live lioness, with pride in the arch of her spine, elegance in how she teased and enticed. She created an up-and-down stroke, just to let him know who was boss…and it wasn't him.

"Rosemary?"

"Sh."

"I'm so in love with you."

"If you talk and interrupt this moment, Whit, I swear I'll never forgive you."

"No more talking," he agreed, and yeah, he noticed she hadn't responded when he admitted being in love with her. But he didn't need her to return an answer or a feeling. Not then. He needed to give her the gift of it. Love. Free and clear.

Her guttural cry of release triggered his. He lasted long enough to give her a second spin, to revel in her after-spasms, the liquid in her breathing. The deep sighs from both of them seemed to define sated. Neither one could talk for a bit. He couldn't, for sure. Just wanted to hold her for the next hundred years, just like this— or at least until they both regained some lung power.

She was the one who managed to talk first. "I have to be killing you."

"You are. You did."

He couldn't see her smile in the darkness, but he could feel it. "I meant, you have to be uncomfortable. You're holding all my weight."

"Oh, that. It's okay. I lost all circulation a while back. But believe me, I don't mind."

She pressed a chuckle on his throat, a soft, devilish kiss. "You don't think the girls will find it odd if they find us locked together in the morning, unable to move, in this, um, definitely compromising position?"

"That'd be a problem," he agreed. "Which means we definitely need to move before six in the morning. Not that they get up that early. But being Christmas, I suspect they won't sleep in like normal."

"You don't think we need sleep ourselves?"

"I do. Right now I'm desperate for sleep. But I'm even more desperate to keep my arms around you."

"You're a darling, Whit."

"Now where did that come from?"

"From me. I thought this was going to be a terrible holiday. Instead, it's turned into one of the best Christmases I've ever had. Because of you."

He wanted to pursue that thought, but she abruptly shifted, threatened all future generations when she climbed off him. Then she started laughing, because her elbow touched something and they both heard the crash of something lightweight and metal hit the floor.

"We're both crazy!" she said. "What on earth were we thinking?!"

He knew what he was thinking. That he was acting like a lovesick calf. He'd wanted to be her Christmas present…only not exactly. He'd wanted her to want him. To see how they were together. How they could be.

He knew, perfectly well, that they'd only known each other for such a short time. Also that his girls were a critical factor in any relationship he took on—and even though they were nuts for Rosemary, that wasn't a guarantee that they could instantly work well as a family. They lived in different places. He knew all that.

And he'd never believed in anyone who instantly fell in love.

But that's how he felt.

Right or wrong, common sense or not, rational or not…he knew she was the right woman for him. The perfect woman for him. A woman he could love the way he'd never loved before.

But he wasn't sure if he could make Rosemary see it. They were both running out of time.

"Listen, you," he said gently.

"What?"

"If you could stay up a few more minutes, let's pour one more glass of wine and meet under the tree in, say… five minutes or so? I just want to tell you something. I promise, it won't take long."

Rosemary cleaned up in the bathroom, pulled on an old, thick robe—the only one she had at the lodge, and then, unfortunately, caught her expression in the mirror. There was a *fat* smile on her mouth. Her eyes were dreamy, drugged. And her face had this absolutely happy look.

Spending even a second more time with Whit Cochran tonight was completely dumb. She should never have agreed. But…she had.

And when she wandered back into the living room, she felt her tension ease. Whit was sitting on the floor with his back to her. He motioned for her to take the reverse position—so she was sitting with her back to him.

"I'm not sure this will work, but I figured we have a chance of behaving if we can't see each other."

"I figured you'd take one look at this ratty old robe and wonder what you ever saw in me."

He poured the wine—a half glass for each, as if promising they weren't staying up long enough to drink more than that. "I know what I saw in you. And see in you. Trust me, the robe's no deterrent." He rubbed her back with his back, making her smile, and she started to relax.

The night had turned quiet as a hush. The fire had gobbled up logs, and become a thick blanket of glowing orange coals. Her body still felt the lushness of Whit's lovemaking, his tenderness, his care, her impossibly strong response to him…but he didn't mention that.

He leaned his head back against her head, said quietly, "You shared something hard and uncomfortable to talk about, when you brought up your ex-fiancé. I'd like to tell you something the same way. Something that needs to stay between the two of us."

"Sure."

"The girls can't know this, Rosemary."

She wanted to turn, when she heard the gravely tone in his voice. She understood he wanted to talk about something difficult for him. But…he'd chosen the sitting arrangements. Maybe because it was easier to say something when he couldn't see her face.

"Here's the thing," he said. "Zoe and I married straight out of school. I couldn't keep my hands off her, never doubted that it was the real kind of love. Her family put on a big wedding, all the trimmings, she looked like an angel. The honeymoon, though, only lasted about three days."

"Uh-oh."

"She liked to tell her friends that I was a work in progress. She thought marrying a landscape architect meant that I'd have a desk job, make good money, come home and we'd do operas and ballet and attend a lot of fancy functions. Fund-raisers. Charity events. Causes. Black-tie stuff."

"Uh-oh," she murmured again.

"I managed to meet one of her expectations. I made good money. It wasn't that hard, because I love the work. It's just that planning a site is only a small part of the job. I pick the plants, the trees and I want to put them in myself, work with the growth sites, the shape of the land, the contours…. I mean, all that stuff is the joy of it."

"You'd love my oldest brother, Tucker. He can get dirty by just stepping outside."

"Yeah. That's me, too. I'd come home, tired to beat the band, and I couldn't even walk in the door. If she had her way, I'd have stripped outside and gotten hosed down before coming in. We had a white couch. White carpeting. Some magazine did a spread of the place. Not because we were that wealthy. But because she was so full of taste and style. Or that's what the article said."

Whit started to rub against her back again, but then he just let out an earthy sigh, and crashed. He was beat. She understood. She was too darned tired to sit any longer, too. Still, they both choose to lie near the hearth, head to head rather than close enough to hold each other. This wasn't about temptation anymore, she understood. It was about him getting something off his mind.

"Okay," she said. "So how'd the marriage go from there?"

"That's exactly what I wanted to tell you. But it isn't really a fun thing to say."

"You think my telling you about George's sexual escapades was fun?"

"No. I think it was damned tough. And that's why I'd like to own up to something on the tough side for me. I was proud of her, Rosemary. What Zoe did, she did so well. I was the screw-up. I went to the ballet, did my best not to fall asleep. I'd do the tux thing, the charity auction thing. I didn't want to argue with her. I didn't want her to be unhappy. If she wanted quiche and I wanted meatloaf, hey, that was no big sacrifice. But the whole package got harder and harder. I just couldn't be the man she wanted."

"Aw, Whit."

"I don't know who screwed up worse—her or me. Maybe she thought I was someone else when she married me. But I was working more and more hours, just to stay away from the house that wasn't my house, the life that wasn't any kind of life I wanted. Only then... she got pregnant."

"Planned?" Rosemary asked.

"Not exactly. Neither of us believed bringing kids into a bad marriage was a good idea. But...we slept together. Not as often as before, but there were always some nights when we'd turn to each other. When the pregnancy test came back, we were both startled. When further testing revealed she was pregnant with twins, well..."

"You were both scared witless?"

"You said it. But...then the girls were born.. and from that moment on, everything was completely different. I took one look at those baby girls and fell like a brick. I always liked kids. But this was like...sunstruck. I never expected a bond that fierce, that powerful, that just plain instinctive. And Zoe...well, we didn't fight anymore. We didn't have time. She had help in the house, but twins are still a lot of work. I may not have had the same parenting ideas that she had...but we got along. I would have stayed in the marriage. Hell, I would have done anything to keep the family together for the girls' sake."

"There's a 'but' in your voice," she said softly.

"I never wished her harm. I swear."

"You don't have to swear. I believe you."

"This whole past year, I've felt so much guilt. I never wanted her to die. Never wanted anything bad to happen to her. But there was this feeling of...relief. Week by week, I felt like I was learning to breathe again. To not live 'tight' all the time. I could laugh out loud.

Come in from work on a hot summer day and pop the top on a beer."

"You felt free," Rosemary said.

"I did. I do. But I know the girls think I'm still grieving for their mom, and I can't—would never—tell them otherwise. They loved her. They miss her.

"Zoe was never evil or bad or anything like that. We just didn't fit. I never put her down in front of them. I never will."

"I understand, Whit."

"Yeah, I think you do. Because you felt you had to keep a secret from family. Different reasons, different situations. But that one aspect is the same. When you love someone, you don't want to hurt them. And if that means you have to lie or keep secrets or whatever, you just do it."

"Whatever you have to do," she agreed.

"I don't like lying. Or to feel like I'm a liar."

"I completely understand, Whit. I never wanted my family to think I'd walk out on a wedding on a whim. But…"

"You felt it'd hurt them more if you told them the truth."

She closed her eyes. It was odd—and maybe amazing—how different their stories were. Yet how much they somehow understood each other.

Whit said nothing for a while. Moments passed. When the old chime clock in the far corner hit twice, she realized he'd fallen asleep. And it was past time both of them got up to their separate bedrooms and knocked off some serious z's.

She meant to get up. Meant to wake Whit. But the

night had been precious in so many ways, that she just didn't want to give in yet. There were still sounds and smells and treasures to inhale. Including Whit.

Espccially including Whit.

And that thought was the last thing she remembered.

Chapter Twelve

When Whit opened his eyes, two bright faces loomed over him. He strongly suspected the chances of further sleep wouldn't make bookie odds.

"Dad, did you and Rosemary really sleep down here? On the floor like this? Weren't you cold?"

"Dad, there are presents under the tree. You told us we weren't doing any presents this year. Except that you bought all that stuff for our rooms. But you said that wasn't about Christmas and it was all getting shipped home. So what'd you get us? Can we open them?"

"Dad, we have to call Grandma and Grandpa. You think it's too early?"

"Dad—"

"Dad—"

He swiped the sleep from his eyes, recognized that his entire body had been twisted in a cold, cramped position, and swung to a sitting position. Then, looking at his girls, raised his arms.

They swooped in for a Christmas hug. They both snugged in close, and both seemed to decide the attire for the morning required red tops with lots of glitter, jeans, and red-and-white socks. They'd brushed their hair, used a red, white and green elastic band to make ponytails, and somewhere, somehow, they'd found some eye makeup.

At least he was pretty sure Lilly's eyelids weren't green—and Pepper's weren't red—when they'd gone to sleep last night.

The questions continued. There was no point in trying to answer any until they'd both run out of steam. In the meantime, he turned a sharp eye on the crumpled mound still on the floor. It didn't look like a body. It looked like someone—such as himself—had half woken in the night, and scooped all the afghans and throws from the couches to cover her up.

She was still covered up, including her head.

She wasn't still sleeping, because that was inconceivable with the girls' racket. But considering how little sleep they'd gotten the night before, he wasn't surprised she was trying to fake it.

That, of course, didn't last long. The girls pounced, peeled the blanket off her face, and discovered a smiling Rosemary—who burst out with a "Happy Christmas, you two!"

They shrieked in return.

"Okay guys, we're going to give Rosemary a chance to run upstairs and change clothes, while I make breakfast."

"He's going to make crepes, Rosemary—but that just means pancakes, don't be worried."

"Hey," Whit objected, trying to sound mightily offended. "I brought my copper pan, the Bisquick, the rum. Not like I don't know how to do this."

Lilly, like always, rushed to reassure her. "Yeah, he uses rum, Rosemary, but it's not like you'll feel funny or get drunk or anything. It just takes a tablespoon. But it has to be good rum."

"Like you'd know good rum from bad," Pepper said, then rolled her eyes.

"Girls…" He took that moment to intervene. "Where'd you find the eye shadow?"

"We already had it."

He had the batter made by the time Rosemary popped downstairs, wearing jeans and a white sweater with Christmas trees. Her eyes met his, with an expression so vulnerable, so fragile…so much worry. And then not. "Hey, I really need to call my parents. Is it too late to do it before breakfast?"

"No, go for it. I need to make a call to the kids' grandparents, too."

They both headed for their cell phones. He called his parents—the time change to Washington was always an issue, but no problem to call them early, because they were always up at the crack of dawn. They loved to talk with the girls.

By the time Whit rang off, he aimed back to the kitchen to finish making breakfast.

Rosemary ambled into the kitchen moments later. "I didn't get my parents yet—their line was busy. But they'll call back any minute. I'll set the table."

Her cell drummed on, just as she scooped up a handful of forks and knives. He poured her coffee, then went back to his flapjacks. Or pancakes. Or crepes. Whatever they were. Since Rosemary'd already made that super coffee cake, it didn't much matter if his pancakes worked out.

He could hear Rosemary from the doorway, as she set the table.

"Dad!" Her voice was bright as sunshine. "Good, good, glad Mom can come on, too. Merry Christmas to you both! When are Ike and Tucker and the kids coming over?"

Some sort of chitchat bantered back and forth. He couldn't hear what her parents said—or guess which parent was talking to her—but from the conversation, it appeared that both her parents poured on guilt with all the enthusiasm of alcohol for an alcoholic.

"I'm sorry, but that's just not going to happen. There's no possibility of any kind that George and I will get back together."

Silence again. He had to flip the first set of crepes, put a fresh dollop of butter in the copper skillet. He missed some of the conversation, but heard her respond to one of her parents.

"That's not really true. I'm doing work up here. For positive, I'm not hiding out at the lodge because I'm afraid to face George or anyone else. I…"

More silence. He couldn't stand it, and took the pot in the dining room to refill her mug. The table was set and she'd plunked down in a chair, her elbow on the table and a hand in her hair.

"Listen, you two. I love you both. I'll be seeing you

in a matter of days. And I'm sorry that you're upset with me. I'm sorry that you feel disappointed. But all I can say is that both of you, by now, should know that you can trust me. Trust my judgment. You should know that I broke up with him for serious reasons. And I really don't want to talk about this again. I hope you both have a super day. Say hi to the gang. And I'll see you in a few days, as soon as I can head down the mountain."

When she clicked off, she tilted her head, saw him in the doorway holding the spatula. Her expression changed, from looking crushed and vulnerable...to a wry smile. "Boy, was that fun."

"That's just what I was thinking. Maybe after breakfast, we could both...I don't know...fall off a cliff. Or go kick up some copperheads. Or put our hands into a beehive."

"Darn it. You're making me laugh."

"You want laughter? Wait until you taste these crepes."

The girls descended on the table. Lilly, thankfully, always ate the burned ones, and Pepper, just as predictably, gobbled them up until she groaned, she was so full. Rosemary expressed shock that they actually tasted good, requiring him to pretend to punch her arm.

Then came the presents. He hung back, tense, watching the girls open their cameras, and all the gear and supplies that came with them. He worried, always, whether he'd picked something age-appropriate...but also something they'd personally like. They were old enough to be into labels and clothes styles that he had no way to cope with.

Rosemary, on the floor near his knee, shot him a glance. "I told you so."

"They do like 'em, don't they."

"Are you kidding? *We love them!*"

Whit got buried in hugs and kisses, but all too soon the girls settled down. Too soon, they noticed the one last present under the tree. For Rosemary. From him.

He'd never run from a problem or a tough challenge, but he had the brief, sick wish that he could just disappear. He hadn't known what to get her. Going into stores and shops, nothing jumped out at him. He had no idea whether to get her something funny, or something traditional, or candles or jewelry or clothes, and every store he'd tried in Greenville, some saleslady took one look at him and started in with the advice. He'd never had a panic attack, but he'd come close.

It mattered. That he do something right. In her eyes, on her terms. It mattered more than he could breathe. He wasn't so good with words, like some men. And God knew, Zoe had told him over and over that he was terrible at choosing presents.

The girls brought the box out from under the tree. They were already rolling their eyes. Okay, so the big box looked a little ragged. He'd had to use a lot of Scotch tape. And he didn't have enough paper, so he'd sort of had to add newspaper to it. And then the bow got crushed when it was upside down in the car.

"What on earth...?" Rosemary asked.

"Listen. It's like I told you before. I get presents all wrong. So don't worry if you don't like it or it's wrong or something. Don't expect anything. Don't—"

"Sh," she told him sternly. Inside the big box was a

smaller box. And then another. And finally, was a manila envelope.

She slit open the envelope, and even before she'd pulled out the sheath of papers, the girls rounded on him.

Lilly was almost beside herself. "*Dad!* You were supposed to get her a real present!"

Pepper was more vocal. "Come on, Dad, what'd you do? Paper isn't a present!"

He couldn't answer them for that instant. His gaze was glued to her profile, as she studied the content on the papers. Finally, she lifted her face to his. She started to say something, stopped. Tried again. Her voice barely reached a whisper.

"Whit. How could you do this to me?"

He saw her eyes well up with tears, felt his heart drop like a stone. The girls got even more upset. "What did you *do* to make Rosemary cry? What's going on, Dad? What did you give her?"

An alien suddenly invaded her body. Rosemary didn't cry. She'd never worn emotions on her sleeve, never lost control in public. But the sting of salty tears in her eyes turned on like a switch that wouldn't shut off. She said quickly to the girls, "I'm not really crying, girls. Honest. I… Something…"

Well, she couldn't finish. She could see the look of alarm and worry on their faces, but she couldn't speak. Her throat suddenly felt as thick as molasses.

Whit carefully, calmly intervened. "You know what? I think holidays get crazy for everyone. Let's give Rosemary a little break, guys. We'll go outside, take your cameras, try 'em out."

She couldn't look at him. She wanted to reassure him, immediately, what his present meant to her. But for at least that moment, her throat was still jammed up, the tears still threatening a hurricane deluge. It was stupid and she was mad at herself, but there it was.

By the time Whit and the girls came back in, she still hadn't figured out what had happened to her, but it was better. Everything was better.

She made a joke to the girls about being an idiot sometimes, and the group congregated in the kitchen. Whit took on breakfast cleanup—and clove-studding the ham. She and the girls put together a cherry sauce, and then a huge batch of the cheesy potatoes the girls wanted.

She tried to catch Whit's eye—wanted and needed to explain why she'd reacted so strongly to his present. But the girls hovered like guardian angels, outside, inside, wherever she was.

She found Pepper waiting outside when she opened the door to the bathroom.

"Listen, Rosemary," Pepper said with a wary eye down the hall as if her sister or dad might appear any minute. "You have to understand about my dad. He doesn't know how to give presents to grown women. My mom said so all the time. She used to say, 'Just give me a check, honey. It'll save you having to shop or buying anything crass. Or trashy.' Or something like that. So it's not like he doesn't try, you know? He gets us. He gets kids. But you're another adult, you know?"

Rosemary opened her mouth, then closed it. When

Whit told her about his marriage last night, all the things the girls had mentioned about their mom suddenly added up. The stories she'd heard about Zoe suddenly all had a different interpretation. Zoe had been a harper. An overcritical badger. Especially of men, but also of her daughters.

That made it all the more important that she catch Whit alone for a few minutes, but she just couldn't make it happen.

Once dinner was in the oven, Whit dragged them all outside again—they'd forgotten to check on their manger, and both girls wanted to take pictures of the crèche. The kids pranced and danced outside, singing off-key renditions of their favorite carols, and coaxing her to sing with them—at least until they arrived at the manger.

Their manger was unrecognizable. The lean-to shelter had leaned over and crashed. The wind had whipped around their sheet people. Some critter had stolen the blanket from the crèche.

"You know what?" Rosemary said, when the kids' exuberance suddenly bottomed out.

"That it was never as great as we thought?" Lilly asked mournfully.

"No. I think what we created was a moment in time. A Christmas Eve moment in time. A moment that no one else was meant to see or hear, exactly the way we did. So we four have the memory of it…but no one else ever will. It's just for us."

Whit looked at her. She felt his gaze, felt the warmth of his eyes. But the girls looked at her as if she'd said something deep and profound and they were trying to figure it out. Finally Lilly stepped forward, and put an arm around her waist.

"Rosemary," she said tactfully, "I think you're really goofy sometimes. But we love you anyway."

"Hey, I love you, too," Pepper said, and took up roost on her other side. Whit came up from behind, and flapped her on the head with a glove...not the most romantic gesture.

"Me, too, on thinking you're goofy," he said gravely. "But also that you probably can't help it."

The twins turned on him, all giggles again. They chased through the woods for a while longer—even though a drizzly rain began—until everyone finally tired. If there was time before dinner, the girls wanted to play a game—something with dice and pretend money, that required a great deal of groaning, moaning and other dramatics. Every time she tried to meet Whit's eye, the girls were engaging him in something or another. Every time she caught him looking at her, and she started to say something—a scream from the girls diverted them both.

Midafternoon, the ham was done. The scramble to the table was akin to heathen wolves who'd been starving in the desert for a half century, and Rosemary told them so.

"Now, Rosemary," Whit said, "I don't think we're *that* bad."

"Well, you wolves have to wait for a minute, because I have something to say."

"Oh, yeah," Pepper said. "We need to say grace."

"Good idea," Whit affirmed.

Rosemary raised her hand. "I agree, too, but first—

I just want to say that I have a sort of present for you girls, but it isn't something I could wrap. I know you're going home to Charleston in a few days. You want to see your friends, get back to school and all that good stuff. But when you get more into your cameras and taking pictures...I'm inviting you to spend a weekend with me up here. You say whenever it works for you. And I'll show you how to develop the pictures yourselves."

"Oh, wow. That's *awesome,* Rosemary!" Pepper skidded around the chairs to give Rosemary a massive hug.

A glass of milk tipped over.

The ham fork clattered to the floor.

Then Whit came up with a toast—a milk toast—before they sliced the ham. "To Rosemary. Who's made this an incredibly special Christmas for all of us."

She lifted her glass. "To all of you," she said, "for making this an incredible Christmas for me."

Out of nowhere, she suffered another massive soft lump in her throat. It had been fun. The whole day. Every bite, every joke, every goofy carol, every witless game and dropped fork. But somehow, by the time she handed out slices of the coconut cake...she felt as if her heart was breaking.

They were leaving her, of course. Not in a matter of weeks, but a matter of a day or two.

If she'd fallen in love—even if she'd fallen out of her mind in crazy love with Whit—he was leaving. He had a job, a life. The girls had their friends, their school, their lives.

A woman would have to be stupid to make something more of the holiday than it was.

Yeah, it was magical. And special. And unique. But it was going to be over, and she needed to toughen up and face it.

She wrapped up the leftover ham and turned toward the kitchen.

"Nope," Whit said. "You did the lion's share of the work. The three of us will do KP. Out. Put your feet up."

"I don't mind—"

"Girls," Whit said, which worked like a trigger on a gun. The girls immediately rushed her, hustled her out of the kitchen, pushed her onto the couch and put a corny Christmas movie on the flat screen.

"Don't move until my dad says," Pepper warned her.

She tried to obey. She meant to obey. But she'd just settled into the dumb movie, when out of the complete blue, a thundering army showed up at her front door.

Bodies hurled inside. Boys. Adults. A howling bloodhound. A very, very pregnant lady. All yelling Merry Christmases and talking at once.

Whit let the girls loose once the dishwasher was filled up, but some baking pans still needed some work. His mind was on Rosemary, not the sink filling up with white soapsuds.

His present idea had been dumb, dumb, dumb. The kind of classic dumb he specialized in with women. He didn't exactly know why it brought tears to her eyes, but he knew the last thing he'd wanted was to stress her. Or upset her. Or hurt her.

She'd seemed fine the rest of the day—and that was true for all of them—but there'd been endless hours without having a single chance to explain about the present. Or discover why it upset her so much in the first place.

He lifted the potato pan into the sudsy water, then looked around for some kind of scrubbing device... when a noisy commotion erupted in the living room. Visitors.

He grabbed a dish towel to wipe his hands and headed for the doorway. Formal introductions were made—none of which could he hear—but he didn't need the introductions anyway.

The men had to be Rosemary's brothers—Tucker and Ike. Both were tall and lean, with Rosemary's eyes. Tucker looked a little more wash-and-wear; Ike more determinedly scruffy. The boys hanging by Tucker were a Mutt and Jeff pair; one athletic and the other a little geeky. They had to be close to his girls' age.

A dog was in the midst of everything—a huge blood-hound, with a tail thwacking anything that moved. He barged through the bodies, climbed on the couch and went into a prompt coma. That is, his eyes immediately drooped, while the tail continued to thump.

Two women were part of the group. A pregnant woman emerged from the crowded bodies—a *very* pregnant woman—who charged in the living room, watermelon-size stomach first, hands behind her back, and galloped straight for the bathroom. The other woman was built on the slight side, but had a smile that filled her face, easy joy in her eyes.

All of them had brought a heap of presents for Rosemary. And the boys had brought the presents *from* Rosemary, so they could open them with her there.

Apparently—he heard this in someone's high volume voice—they'd had dinner early at the MacKinnon seniors. The MacKinnon mom/grandma predictably got an emergency call from the hospital. So they'd cleared out, decided to pack up their cars and head for the MacKinnon lodge and Rosemary.

Whit shook a half-dozen hands, met everyone even though he couldn't hear over the din, and watched Rosemary nestle in with her obviously loved and loving kin. At some point the bloodhound realized there were two other kids in the house—the twins—and uncrumpled from the couch to meet them, slobber all over them and get hugged. The kids, boys and girls both, took one look at each other and abruptly turned into wall huggers. Ike's wife, Ginger, noticed the kids were gripped by a terrible case of shyness, and came through with a rum cake.

Both the rum cake and last of the white coconut cake were devoured. Xmas cookies were produced. Presents ripped open. Soft drinks were handed out in the living room. And somewhere around an hour or two later, Whit headed for the refrigerator...when he abruptly discovered Rosemary's two brothers right behind him.

Tucker had a bottle of Carolina Peach Shine. The whiskey had a reputation; it was legal moonshine but that hadn't always been the case. There were still stills up and down the mountains in this part of Carolina. Tucker explained that history, while Ike amiably produced three glasses.

So...Whit didn't need a sledgehammer to get the message. Ike and Tucker took their big brother roles seriously—which meant he was about to get a grilling.

* * *

Rosemary knew the instant she saw her brothers' faces that she needed to save Whit, and quickly. When the MacKinnons first showed up, she saw no reason to worry. Whit ambled right in the middle of it all.

Garnet, Tucker's wife, had brought gifts—vanilla—from her own private vanilla stock. Whit caught on that she was the owner of Plain Vanilla, an herb store down-mountain. Garnet tended to hang back from strangers, but not with Whit, who immediately coaxed her into a dialogue about how she grew the vanilla, her techniques and ideas. Once Whit mentioned being a landscape architect, Rosemary doubted even a machete could pry them apart. Fertilizers. Weed killers. Soil pH levels. They buzzed on about stuff that clearly thrilled them both.

Tucker shot her an amused look. He loved to see his new wife open up and blossom.

The boys finally got to open presents from their aunt Rosemary—and naturally, she'd felt duty bound to choose things their parents wouldn't appreciate. Drums. A chemistry set. An ant farm. But a couple things were a little more serious. She'd bought Pete some modest shares of stock in a respected toy manufacturer, because he was born for business, even at his young age. And Will got a rock tumbler, which was another truly horrible noisemaker intended to drive his parents crazy.

Tucker showed his appreciation by bopping her on the head several times. Ike initially gave her a kiss and a shrug-hug, but then he hunkered down with the kids. The girls and boys were still a little frozen with each other, but Ike got them loosened up by telling bear stories.

En route, Rosemary had to catch up with Ginger, Ike's new bride. Ginger had met Ike when she was in a heap of trouble—her so-loved grandfather had developed Alzheimer's; the family tea plantation had been self-destructing; her ne'er-do-well father showed up, assuming she'd be happy to support him…and oh, yeah, she happened to be pregnant by a man she described as a cross between vermin and a louse.

Ginger, unlike her gentler sister-in-law, never had to be coaxed to talk. She was redoing an antique bassinet for the baby.… Her grandfather was doing far better with family in the house…and she was far, far, far too pregnant to handle the crisis of her deadbeat dad, so she'd passed that crisis on to her new husband.

"Everyone who meets Ike," Ginger told her, "thinks he's laid back and easygoing and not one to walk fast in a tornado."

"I know," Rosemary agreed, half an eye on Whit, who was still talking to Garnet, but simultaneously managed to move a dish of cookies away from the bloodhound's mournful eyes. "Ike always claimed to be lazier than a slug. I think he just really didn't want to be work-obsessed like our parents."

"Well, that's the scam he sold himself. Anyway, he met my father, couldn't have been more welcoming or nicer. Next thing, he took my blood pressure and then just said that my dad could always visit, but he wasn't living with us at this time. I told him that was fine. Next thing I know, he's put my father to work, doing lists and inventories of the tea supplies. My dad took off at the speed of light."

Rosemary chuckled, well able to imagine that picture. "Boy or girl, or do you know that?" She noticed Ginger's hand suddenly press on her bulging abdomen.

"The ultrasound claims it's a girl. Which has made Ike over the moon…but I have a nightmare worrying she'll be a redhead with a temper like mine. And my other nightmare is worrying that there are twins in there. How can I possibly be this big if there's only one?"

"You're not *that* big," Rosemary promised her.

"I am. I feel like my name should be synonymous with whales. Elephants. Defunct dinosaurs. I haven't seen my feet in a month. Thank God for Garnet."

Garnet finally disengaged from Whit and moved closer. "I've been giving her herbs and herbal teas. Not medicinally. She doesn't need medicine. But just to boost her spirits."

"How can my spirits get boosted if I'm so fat I can't see my feet?"

Ike showed up from behind her back. "Have you ever seen a sexier, more desirable woman in your life?" He kissed her on the crown of her head.

"You can't mean that. You're delusional." But she looked at him with pure, naked love in her eyes.

Garnet rolled her eyes at Rosemary. "I thought Tucker and I were bad. But these two can't seem to let up on the google-eyes."

"I love seeing my brothers brought low," Rosemary assured them both.

The kids came pouring through the door. She started

cleaning up one mess—all the Christmas wrappings—only one of the kids spilled a bowl of nuts, and then dishes and glasses reproduced at the speed of sound on all surfaces.

By the time she realized the women and children were all in the living room and the men were alone in the kitchen, she almost had a heart attack. Her brothers had cornered Whit, she just knew it. She climbed over Ginger's knees, weaved past the kids—all of whom were eating popcorn from the tree—and galloped toward the kitchen doorway.

Ike and Tucker were just exiting—a bottle of moonshine in Ike's hand. Opened bottle of moonshine. Alarm drummed in her pulse. "What have you done, you two?" she asked darkly.

"It's okay. We just need to see you for a minute."

"Why. What's wrong. Where's Whit—"

"We were all outside for just a couple minutes." Tucker, the eldest, had always used his strength to muscle her into doing what he wanted. Of course, that was how she'd learned to pinch and bite.

"What's going on?"

"We're going to the bathroom."

"Together? Do we have to?"

"We only want two seconds alone with you. It's the only place where we can't be overheard."

"What if I'd rather have witnesses?"

"This is between the three of us. Besides. If we're taking over a bathroom, you can be positive we won't talk for over three minutes. Ginger can barely wait that long between visits, and she's not about to waddle all the way upstairs."

"Where's Whit *now?*" she repeated. "How much moonshine did you pour down him?"

"Rosemary, Rosemary. How could you think such thoughts about your brothers? I swear you won't be mad at us. We just want to tell you a couple things in private."

They were evil, both of them. Always had been, always would be. But to give them credit, they were brief. They locked the door, looked at her portentously, gave big slow sighs—but once she punched them, they both started talking.

"Okay, here's the deal." Tucker spoke first. "We approve. We came here, both of us prepared to mop the floor with him if we had to. But I think you've finally met your match, cookie."

That was all he had to say, and Ike took even less time. "I'll never ask you again about George. Don't care. He doesn't matter. You've moved on. And to a better guy than George ever was."

"That's *it?* You're not even going to ask my opinion? You don't know what's happening or not happening. You don't know—"

"We know enough."

"Except…" Tucker stuck his hands in his pockets. "I was wondering if Whit's girls might like to come home with us. Just for the night. The kids were all talking about some game they wanted to play."

Rosemary frowned. "It wouldn't be up to me. It'd be up to Whit. But—"

"It's not like we'd be far away, sis. Just down-mountain. If the girls wanted to come back, I could have them back here in less than twenty minutes. I figured we should ask you before asking Whit. And before bringing it up to the kids."

"Well, I—"

"We could hear the four of them talking about this dumb game they wanted to play. You know how big our place is. It's not as if we don't have a whole wing to separate the genders."

"That never crossed my mind," Rosemary said, unsure why the brothers were sharing meaningful looks, and she got the feeling she was being manipulated. She didn't think it was necessarily a bad idea; she just felt railroaded.

"For that matter, if they just want to play the game and then come back up here with you and Whit, that'd be fine, too. It's no problem either way."

When Tucker was being nice, there was always a reason. She wanted to object on that basis— Tucker's historical record—only she couldn't really think of any real reason why the kids couldn't play a game together if they all wanted to.

"Ask Whit," she said.

They did. The commotion abruptly turned back into a noisy crescendo, with kids running around, collecting hats and mittens or forgetting them and coming back. Shoes were lost. Then found. Ginger, once she stood up, needed a bathroom run. Before she left, ten minutes later, she needed another one. Pansy, the bloodhound, came out of her coma and wove her way between people, especially people who were trying to carry things to and from cars. The girls were talking in shrieks, which, come to think of it, Rosemary had long figured out was their regular speaking voice.

Over and through it all, she kept track of Whit, and outside when the crew was all leaving, she noticed her two brothers aim toward Whit.

She galloped in front of Whit at breakneck speed. Stood in front of him, folded her arms.

Tucker and Ike stopped dead, glanced at Whit, then at her...and then both of them started laughing like hyenas.

"Whether you like it or not, Whit, it looks like she's going to protect you from us."

"If you two don't start being nice to me, I'd hate to tell you what I'll be giving the kids next Christmas. I'm thinking a boa constrictor. In a cage with a loose lock."

That didn't help. They laughed even harder.

To make matters worse, she suddenly felt Whit's hands on her shoulders from behind. "It's okay," he whispered. "I appreciate your protecting me. They're pretty scary."

"You think they're funny, but you weren't their little sister."

"I get that. But I like how they treat their little sister."

"That's only because you can't help it. You have that same twisted Y chromosome. You're not responsible for occasional Neanderthal opinions."

"Whew. I'm relieved you don't find me responsible."

The whole time she was having this insane conversation with him, his hands were still on her shoulders from behind, and the cars were backing up, lights on, disappearing down the mountain. Heaven knew when night had come on, but the sky was muddy black, clouds blustering against each other and occasionally spitting.

Obviously they needed to head inside, but she wasn't

ready. She wasn't ready for nightfall, for all the sudden silence.

And she definitely wasn't ready to face Whit.

Chapter Thirteen

"You realize that your brothers set us up so we could be alone tonight," Whit said.

"I know. They're both as subtle as sledgehammers." Cold rain kept drooling from the sky. Silver drops slid in her hair. In her eyes.

But she was intensely aware that something was different about Whit. He didn't seem to notice the cold, the dark, the rain. He just kept looking at her. There was a calm in his face, in his gaze.

"I told your brothers what I'd given you for Christmas," he mentioned.

"Oh? And what'd they say?"

"Well, once I told them, they stopped trying to pour moonshine down my throat. That peach moonshine..." Whit shook his head. "That's quite a drink. On a par with..."

"Gasoline?"

"That wasn't my first thought, but close enough. Tucker and Ike had been grilling me nonstop. When I confessed about the present, they both stopped talking altogether. They had this crazy idea that you loved the present."

"I did. I do." Blast it. Tears blurred her eyes again. Showing up like they did before, out of the blue, and including a soft thick feeling in her throat. "I more than loved it, Whit."

Slowly, cautiously, he came closer. Used the edge of his thumbs to wipe the spill of tears. "I thought you were crying because I'd disappointed or upset you."

"No. Never that. Just the opposite. It's just...there isn't much that moves me to tears. Not like this." She had to get past that lump in her throat, needed to tell him—wanted to tell him—exactly what his present had meant. "Most of my life, I've thought of myself as kind of invisible. My parents would sometimes forget that they were leaving me alone. My first boyfriend in high school—he was a good guy, no question—but when we broke up, he was with someone else in less than a week. Easy for me to start thinking of myself as forgettable. And then, of course, there was George. George said he loved me. I don't actually doubt that he meant it...but when push came down to shove, apparently he didn't know me at all. Never saw me. Not really."

"You might be giving me a whole lot more credit than I deserve, love. Your brothers just thought you'd like the present."

She laughed, but there was still a lump in her throat. Still the threat of emotional tears. Yet she raised her face to his.

And right there, so easily, his lips were waiting for her. Waiting for the chance to connect, the way Whit connected with her every second since he'd shown up in her life. He offered softness, tenderness.

"It's starting to freeze. And you're cold," he said.

"I don't want to go in yet. I want you to show me… your plan."

He pulled a stocking cap from his jacket pocket. Popped it on her head. Took off his jacket, wrapped it around her…then wrapped an arm around her, as well.

Ignoring dark and chill, snugged tight against him, he explained about the unique gift he'd given her. When she'd opened the envelope, she'd seen the rough sketched drawing of the yard around the lodge…but almost immediately understood what he was giving her and why.

Now, he walked her down to the fork in the road that marked the MacKinnon property, ambled up the drive, motioning and explaining as they went. "It's quite a slope," he said, "and I could see both that the soil tends to be dry, and tends to get a ton of sun. To make the most of both those issues, I'd want to plant into raised beds, do a gravel mulch. The thing about rosemary…"

He looked at her.

"The thing about Rosemary is that she's as close to perfect as anything on earth."

She gulped. "Doggone it, Whit. You're going to make me cry again."

"I don't think so. I'm just telling you the straight truth of the matter. They used to say rosemary was for remembrance. I think that's because she's so unique. No one could forget her. No one would want to forget her. She attracts birds and butterflies, the beautiful and gentle things around her. She's just as pretty in summer as in winter. She's got this fresh, pretty scent that affects everyone and anything around her." He motioned. "I think a hedge type of rosemary would be perfect; she'd greet everyone as they were coming up the drive. Up closer to the house, we could use a ground cover variety, mix up the blue and pink flowers, have a display that welcomes people coming in. Of course, people already know your door is always open to everyone...."

"Whit," she said, but damnation if her eyes weren't watering again.

"Once she's planted, she's extraordinarily self-sustaining. But that isn't to say she wouldn't thrive even more with care and attention. I have this idea about transplanting certain vulnerable plants. You dig the hole, make a nest for the plant, where it's warm and soft and safe. Then you put her in, and kind of 'love her in'—no tools, just your hands. Rosemary isn't a complaining or whining kind of plant, so if she isn't thriving, you need to pay attention. She's strong. She can weather all kinds of trouble. But that's not to say she doesn't need some cherishing, some cosseting, some plain old everyday love. She..."

Okay. He was going to talk all night if she let him. So she swung around in his arms, lifted up, invited a kiss.

Eyes closed, she cherished the mold and meld of his lips on hers. She tasted love. She tasted hope. She tasted the future.

She also stopped for just a second. "Whit. Did I tell you that I love you?"

"Maybe not in exact words."

"I'm glad you figured it out. But I'd still like to use the exact words. I love you, Whit. More and in a different way than I ever expected to love anyone. You know me, the one no one else ever has."

"I need you in my life, the way I've never needed anyone." His eyes had a fierce shine. "Before the new year, I'd like to pick out a ring."

"Before the new year, I would love to wear your ring."

She knew they needed to talk about the girls. About where they would live, and how they could manage and balance their lives. But she wasn't remotely worried that they could come up with solutions, or that they could conquer any and all challenges in front of them.

Right now, all that could wait. She stole another kiss, then took his hand.

"Before we both freeze to death, I'm taking you in the house."

"I'll take you in. Anywhere, anytime," he said. "Merry Christmas, my love."

"And all the Christmases ahead of us."

They both smiled, and aimed for the house.

* * * * *

A sneaky peek at next month…

Cherish™

ROMANCE TO MELT THE HEART EVERY TIME

My wish list for next month's titles…

In stores from 20th September 2013:

☐ The Christmas Baby Surprise — Shirley Jump

& A Weaver Beginning — Allison Leigh

☐ Single Dad's Christmas Miracle — Susan Meier

& Snowbound with the Soldier — Jennifer Faye

In stores from 4th October 2013:

☐ A Maverick for Christmas — Leanne Banks

& Her Montana Christmas Groom — Teresa Southwick

☐ The Redemption of Rico D'Angelo — Michelle Douglas

& The Rancher's Christmas Princess — Christine Rimmer

Available at WHSmith, Tesco, Asda, Eason, Amazon and Apple

Just can't wait?

Wrap up warm this winter with Sarah Morgan...

Sleigh Bells in the Snow

Kayla Green loves business and hates Christmas.

So when Jackson O'Neil invites her to Snow Crystal Resort to discuss their business proposal.. the last thing she's expecting is to stay for Christmas dinner. As the snowflakes continue to fall, will the woman who doesn't believe in the magic of Christmas finally fall under its spell...?

4th October

www.millsandboon.co.uk/sarahmorgan

1013/MB435

She's loved and lost — will she ever learn to open her heart again?

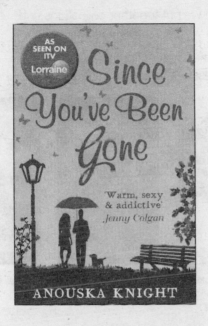

From the winner of ITV Lorraine's Racy Reads, Anouska Knight, comes a heart-warming tale of love, loss and confectionery.

'The perfect summer read — warm, sexy and addictive!'
—Jenny Colgan

For exclusive content visit:
www.millsandboon.co.uk/anouskaknight

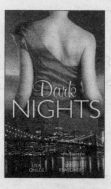
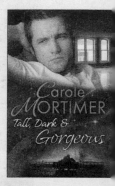

Barbul sept 17